RAGS TO RICHES
Volume One

Remove the Empty Spaces

Close the Distance

T.A. CHASE

Rags to RichesVolume One
ISBN # 978-1-78184-757-2
©Copyright T.A. Chase 2014
Cover Art by Posh Gosh ©Copyright 2014
Interior text design by Claire Siemaszkiewicz
Totally Bound Publishing

Published in 2014 by Totally Bound Publishing, Newland House, The Point, Weaver Road, Lincoln, LN6 3QN, United Kingdom.

Totally Bound Publishing is an imprint of Total-E-Ntwined Limited.

REMOVE THE EMPTY SPACES

Dedication

Thank you to those who read the first draft of this story, and saw the potential for more.

Chapter One

"I want you all to fucking think of a fucking solution."

It was going to be one of those days, Ion thought, as he pushed his mail cart off the elevator onto the executive floor.

"Why the fuck do I pay you bastards such fucking ridiculous salaries if you can't come up with one fucking good idea?"

Ion winced before sending Patrick, his best friend and Mr Adrien Bellamy's executive assistant, a sympathetic grin. "Sounds like he's in rare form today."

"You have no idea. Bellamy's been like this all morning."

Adrien Bellamy was the CEO and President of Bellamy International, a multi-national company that acquired failing businesses and tried to make them successful again. Well, it was just one branch of the business. Bellamy International had its fingers in several different pies, which suited Ion just fine. He might only be working in the mailroom right now, but he planned on making his way up the corporate ladder to a troubleshooting position someday.

Ion was ambitious, and it was his drive to succeed that had brought him to the company. Bellamy International was one of the top one-hundred businesses in the world. Where better for a young businessman to work?

"All your ideas are shit. I won't lay off a thousand workers simply because the men in charge were fucking greedy crooks. You have to find me a solution that doesn't result in people losing their jobs."

Ion knew better than to ask why Mr Bellamy was furious. Patrick couldn't tell him since being the head man's minion meant he came across a lot of sensitive material, and Patrick could lose his job if he were to share any of it, even with another person in the company.

After handing Patrick some mail, Ion checked his list to see whom else he had to deliver to.

"They're all in the conference room. Have been since this morning when I got here. Bellamy called a meeting of all the execs." Patrick sifted through the large pile of envelopes Ion had given him.

"Why aren't you in there taking notes or whatever he has you do during meetings?"

Patrick shrugged. "Not sure. I sent him a text to see if he needed me for anything. He told me to cancel the rest of his meetings for the day, and work on something else."

They both jumped when a loud crash resounded from the conference room. Ion straightened from where he'd been resting his hip against Patrick's desk. The door flew open then ricocheted back after hitting the wall with force. He and Patrick watched in amazement as Mr Richardson, the CFO, dragged Mr Bellamy out of the room.

"God damn it, Sidney. Why the fuck do I have them here if they can't figure out one fucking solution? Monkeys are more intelligent than that group." Mr Bellamy yanked his arm out of Mr Richardson's grip. He paced the length of Patrick's office area.

Ion had left his cart next to the elevator, and he found he was happy about that because his boss would've tripped over it. It was wise to stay out of the way when Mr Bellamy was angry, if only because he didn't pay attention to where he was going. After pressing into a corner, Ion hoped no one would notice him.

"They're fucking morons." Mr Bellamy ran his fingers through his hair.

"Patrick, can you call the cleaning crew and get someone to come up here? There's a mess in the conference room." Richardson seemed calm, but then he always did. Ion had never seen the CFO lose his cool in the three years Ion had worked for the company.

Mr Bellamy was the complete opposite. He lost his temper at least once a week, usually at Patrick, then later, Ion would get an earful about what a prick Bellamy was. Yet Mr Bellamy never seemed vicious with his anger. He simply had a short fuse, and intolerance for stupidity.

"Yes, Mr Richardson. I'll make sure it gets cleaned up." Patrick reached for the phone.

"Also, cancel all of Mr Bellamy's appointments for the rest of the day. I'm taking him out of here. He needs to cool down before he ends up firing every person who works for him. I'd hate having to pay them bonuses to make up for his temper tantrum."

"Shut the fuck up, Sidney. I wouldn't threaten to fire them if they'd just do their jobs."

Ion tried hard not to stare as Mr Bellamy passed by him, but it was difficult not to when the head of the corporation could easily be in the running for Sexiest Man Alive. *Christ on a stick!* If Bellamy hadn't been worth a billion dollars or more, he could have made his fortune on the runway as a model.

Bellamy's hair was a pale gold that he wore cut short on the sides and longer on top. His bright blue eyes sparkled with fierce intelligence, and hidden deep inside, a kindness that Ion knew Bellamy rarely showed to anyone.

Ion had happened to see one of Bellamy's random acts of kindness to a homeless woman who had claimed one of the alleys next to the building. Ion had been making his way to work one morning, and he'd spied Bellamy covering the woman with what looked like a brand new blanket.

He had waited until Bellamy left before he'd dropped off the bag of sandwiches he had brought for her. It wasn't much, but Ion had come to learn about the woman's past, and she was a wonderful person who'd fallen down and couldn't get back up on her feet.

Bellamy had nicely tanned skin, speaking of his time spent outdoors, doing all sorts of exciting sports like sailing and rock climbing. Ion got to hear about all those trips from Patrick, who had to book them for Bellamy.

The man's tailored suits were probably hand-made in Italy. Everything Bellamy wore and how he carried himself spoke of money and privilege, yet he knew the names of the people cleaned his office and those in the mailroom. Ion was pretty sure most CEOs wouldn't know anyone they didn't have to deal with on a day-to-day basis.

Oh, Ion knew Bellamy could be arrogant and get into snits when things didn't go his way. Being friends with Patrick gave him an unique insight into Bellamy, but it didn't make Ion dislike Bellamy. In fact, all the contradictions fascinated Ion even more.

"This needs to be fixed before Monday, Sidney. If not, I'm going to have to fire all those people, and I don't want to do that. Not when it wasn't their fault the company was run into the ground. Why do incompetent people always think they can run national businesses?" Bellamy whirled, waving his arms around and hitting Ion in the chest.

Ion froze, really not wanting to be drawn into this discussion. He snorted to himself. Like Bellamy and Richardson would ask a lowly mail clerk his opinion on such an important situation. Even though he didn't know what the problem was, it was obviously to Ion that Bellamy needed it solved quickly.

"Oh Ion, did you have mail to deliver?" Bellamy sent him a distracted smile like his mind was still caught up with his racing thoughts.

"Yes, sir. I dropped some off to Patrick. Just have a few for Mr Richardson." Ion tipped his head to both men before meeting Patrick's gaze and seeing his friend mouth 'Talk to you later.'

Before Mr Bellamy got started, Ion gathered his cart. He grabbed the letters for Mr Richardson, then handed them to the CFO's assistant. Ion rushed to the elevator to push the button. Bellamy, Richardson, and Patrick all stared at him while he focused on the floor numbers lighting up at the top of the elevator. Not wanting to give away his nervousness, he refrained from poking at the button again.

"Come on. Come on," he muttered, wishing that pushing it several times in a row actually did make the elevator go faster.

Ion could almost hear Patrick snickering at him, especially since Patrick had been privy to one of Ion's drunken ramblings about how beautiful Adrien Bellamy was, and how much Ion would love to get that man in bed. Being this close to the man didn't happen to Ion very often, and he was rather flustered, knowing Adrien was watching him.

Finally the elevator arrived, and Ion shoved the mail cart into the car. When he swung around to poke the third floor button, he saw that Adrien and Sidney were gone, and Patrick was propped up against his desk while he laughed.

"Just remember, Patrick, payback's a bitch," Ion shouted as the doors closed. He'd get Patrick back somehow. It would take him a few weekends thinking on it, but he was sure he'd come up with something. After having been best friends with Patrick for ten years, Ion knew the man well.

He finished his rounds, then headed to the basement where the mail room was located. It was time for him to go home, and do some work.

* * * *

Ion slammed his door shut when he got back to his apartment. He had to do some research because he wanted to know more about the company Adrien had been talking about. He wasn't angry about Patrick not telling him because it would've cost Patrick his job if he had said something.

He had an idea which business it was. Bellamy International had just acquired two new companies in the last month. Both of them were struggling, but from what Ion had overheard, only one of them was so bad, Bellamy was considering laying people off.

Ion turned on his computer before rushing to his bedroom. He changed into jeans and a sweatshirt, then went to the kitchen. While his computer finished booting up, he made two meatloaf sandwiches for himself. He was glad his mom had insisted he take some home the other night. It saved him from wasting time going to get something to eat.

As Ion ate, he continued to go over what he'd heard that morning. He kept track of all the companies Bellamy International acquired because the idea of buying struggling companies and deciding whether they could continue, or whether they needed to be closed fascinated him. Ion was privately proud of the fact that Bellamy rarely liquidated the companies they bought. Most of the time, they managed to find ways to make the enterprises viable again.

The only company that fit what Adrien had said was Huntsman Toys, a small family-owned business. Ion had a vested interest in the toy maker since his parents and his older brother all worked there. His parents had always worked on the assembly lines, and his brother was one of the toy designers.

Ion didn't want them to lose their jobs, not when his parents were so close to retiring. Plus his brother had two kids to take care of. His family had been worried when they heard Huntsman was being sold to Bellamy. Ion had tried to reassure them that Bellamy was the best company possible to have bought them.

He'd tried to be upbeat for them, but Ion understood the economy and knew there might be no way for Bellamy to save their jobs. Finding any solution to the problem would help get rid of the knot in the pit of his stomach.

He dug through all the public records he could find. Ion lost track of time as he read and made notes every chance he got. As he worked, several ideas formed in his head, but by the time he was done, he'd discarded all but two of them. He wanted to present two workable ideas that didn't include laying off all the workers to Bellamy on Monday. Yet it took a phone call to his brother, Bogdan, to cement his decision.

"Hey, Bogdan, how are you doing?" Ion leaned back in his chair, staring up at the ceiling.

"I'm doing well, Ion. Are you okay? I don't usually hear from you when we're going to see each other at Mother's on Sunday." Bogdan sounded tired.

Ion chuckled. "I'm fine. I needed to talk to you about something, and didn't want Mother or Pop to overhear."

"You didn't get a girl pregnant, did you?"

Ion tried to ignore the eagerness in his brother's voice. His family didn't understand why he would be gay when there were some very lovely girls out there, just waiting for him to ask. No matter how many times he told them being gay wasn't a choice for him, they still all openly hoped he'd change his mind.

"No, and for the one millionth time, I never will. I need to talk to you about Huntsman." He stood, getting ready to start pacing. Ion discovered he thought best while he moved.

Bogdan sighed, then Ion heard him say something to Olive, his wife. "I'm going to go in the other room to talk to Ion. Don't worry. It won't take long, and I'll be back before it's time for the kids' show."

Ion heard Olive say to tell him hi from her. "Tell Olive, I love her, and I have a great new recipe I'm going to email her later."

He listened to his brother deliver his message, then Bogdan said, "All right. I'm in the kitchen. What did you want to talk to me about?"

"I need you to tell me everything you know about Huntsman Toys, and any new ideas that might have been put on hold when the company was sold." Ion glanced around to see where he'd set his notebook and pen.

Bogdan hummed softly for a moment. "I'm not sure I should be telling you this."

"Did you sign any kind of confidentiality form or anything like that?" Ion didn't want to get his brother in trouble.

"No. I'm not part of the Huntsman board. There's no reason for me to sign one since I don't know anything." Bogdan seemed unsure what Ion wanted from him.

"Fine, then you can tell me everything you know without endangering your job. I'm trying to come up with a way to help you and your fellow workers." He wasn't going to say anything more than that until after he handed in his proposals.

He spent the next twenty minutes telling Ion everything he knew about the company and any designs that might have been in consideration before Huntsman Toys sold, and they were put on hold.

At the end of the time, Bogdan said, "I have to go. It's time for the kids' show, and they like it when I watch it with them."

"Give the boys a kiss from me, and thanks."

"If anyone can figure out how to save our jobs, Ion, you can."

Ion laughed. "I have two nephews to spoil. I need to make good money."

Bogdan chuckled. "True, and they always love seeing what you buy them next."

"I know how to do things, Bogdan. You are in charge of their lives, and I'm not going to step on your toes. Go on and watch TV with your kids. I'll see you at dinner on Sunday. Oh, by the way, don't say anything to Mama and Pops about what we talked about." Ion told his brother. "I don't want to get their hopes up, then have it not work out."

Because it might not, and Ion knew the chances of Adrien taking his suggestions seriously were a million to one, but Ion wanted to try. It was one of the reasons why he was working to put himself through graduate school. He was only a semester away from getting his MBA, and he had plans of getting a job at a Fortune 100 company as a troubleshooter. Finding a way to fix this problem would be a great step toward achieving his goal.

"I won't say a word, Ion. I promise. Now try to get some sleep. You're all excited, so I'm pretty sure you won't be listening to me about this." Bogdan knew him well.

"I'll try, but I can always sleep tomorrow once I get this worked out. Have a good night, Bogdan."

Ion hung up, and started incorporating the information Bogdan had given him into his proposals. He wrote up two separate suggestions, so Adrien and the board had options, even though Ion wanted them to pick only one.

When his cell rang, he glanced up to check the clock. *Holy shit!* It was one in the morning. He'd been working for over seven hours. He'd never worked that long on homework in school.

He picked up his phone when it rang again. Ion saw Patrick's name on his screen, and thought about not answering it. Then he realized Patrick would probably keep calling him until he either turned his phone off or answered the damned thing.

"What do you want?"

"Oh, so you are still alive," Patrick quipped.

"Yes, I'm still alive. Why would you think otherwise?" He frowned.

Patrick snorted. "Maybe because you were supposed to meet me at Harvey's around eleven for drinks and some dancing."

Ion slapped his hand against his forehead. "Shit. I'm sorry, Patrick. I got caught up in something, and totally lost track of time."

"I'm not sure that's a good enough excuse, unless you got caught up in bed with a hot man, and he tied you up or something." Patrick joked.

"I wish," Ion muttered.

"Should I grab some wine, then come up to see what got you so focused, you forgot about drinks?"

Ion thought about telling Patrick, but he wasn't sure that he wouldn't get Patrick in trouble.

"How about you grab some wine, come to see me, and we'll chat about the hot guy you left the club with last weekend? You haven't said anything about him," Ion suggested.

It was the best solution. This way he could still work on his project, then have a nice chat with his best friend. He was getting a little tired of hitting the clubs and picking up strangers to bring home, then kick out of his apartment in the morning.

"I can do that. I'll get some of that white you really liked." There was muffling noises as Patrick must have covered the speaker on his phone.

Ion didn't pay attention to the faint words he heard. Patrick was obviously telling someone he was leaving. Was Patrick with the man he met last weekend or was it someone new? Patrick never seemed to settle down with any one person, and Ion was pretty sure Patrick was getting bored with the same old routine like Ion was.

"I can be there in thirty minutes," Patrick told him.

"You have a key. I might even have some cheese and crackers for us to nibble on. Oh, and I have some of my mother's meatloaf."

He held his phone away from his ear while Patrick squealed. Ion had known that would be the true incentive to getting Patrick to come over. Patrick had an unholy love for Ion's mother's meatloaf.

"I'll be over as quickly as possible. You better not eat the rest of it just to spite me," Patrick warned him.

Ion chuckled. "Don't worry. There's plenty left. I had two sandwiches when I got home, but you know my mom. She sent me home with one whole loaf to myself, and as much as I like her food, I don't need to eat that much of it."

"Well, I do. See you." Patrick hung up.

After ending the call, Ion tossed his phone onto the coffee table before he started to pace. Maybe he should have Patrick go over the project, to see if there was anything he could add that would make Adrien believe in what he had to say.

But Ion came back to the fact that he didn't want Patrick risk losing his job because he'd leaked private company information to Ion. Of course, he hadn't, but Ion doubted anyone would believe them if they said that.

He pursed his lips as he thought about it. There wasn't anyone else he could trust to give him suggestions or anything like that. He would just have to turn the proposals in, and hope for the best.

After his printer spat the papers out, Ion sat down and went through every page, word for word, circling phrases and crossing some out. Patrick came through the door just as Ion finished the last page. He shuffled all the papers into a pile, then set them next to his computer.

Ion took the bottle of wine Patrick held out to him before heading into the kitchen. "You know where the plates are, and how to heat up the meatloaf. I'll pour the wine. I can't believe you only got one bottle of it. So I'm guessing this isn't a get-drunk-and-regret-it kind of night."

Patrick had his head buried in the refrigerator, and his words were muffled.

"What did you say?"

"I said no, it's not. I have an all-day shopping excursion with my sister tomorrow, and I can't be hung over while I deal with her." Patrick pulled out the container holding the meatloaf.

Ion cringed at the thought of having to do anything with Patrick's twin sister, Patrice. She was even higher maintenance than Patrick, and twice as hyper. Ion had spent many a day following the two of them from store to store, and hauling bags full of clothes for them. Both of them were fashionistas, so Ion tried to always be busy when they were doing one of their monthly shopping days.

"Good idea, man. She can be a little unnerving without a hangover." Ion popped the cork before pouring out two glasses of wine. He stuck the bottle in an ice bucket, then carried it out to the living room, along with his glass. "Grab your glass when you're on your way out here."

He flopped onto his couch, staring up at the ceiling while he waited for Patrick to join him. Sipping his wine, he turned his mind off from the project he'd worked on all night. He'd go back, clean it up, then get it printed at a professional printer. He was going to make it look as perfect as he could.

"Humph…your mother's meatloaf…hmmm." Patrick wandered in as he stuffed the forkful in his face.

"God, man, you sound like you're making love to that." Ion burst out laughing, holding his sides as he doubled over.

Patrick flipped him the bird, but didn't stop eating. When he finished, Patrick almost licked the plate clean before curling up next to Ion on the couch.

"Oh my God, I can't believe I ate that much. Why didn't you stop me?" Patrick rubbed his flat stomach.

"I wasn't about to come between you and Mother's meatloaf. Dude, you would've taken my arm off or something." Ion took another drink of wine, then patted Patrick's arm. "Tell me why you decided to come over here instead of staying at the club. Don't get me wrong. I'm always glad to hang out with you, but staying in on a Friday night without sex being involved has never really been your thing."

Patrick slowly slid to the side until his head rested on Ion's shoulder. "We're getting old, aren't we?"

Ion blinked, not used to Patrick talking about his age or sounding so sad. "Yes, we are. I'm twenty-seven, and you're twenty-six. We were never going to stay young forever."

"I know, but honey, I was hoping we would. I'm getting bored with the whole scene. I guess I realized hanging out, drinking wine with my best friend is more fun than wedging myself up to a bar in a crowded club where most of the men don't want a relationship. All they're looking for is a one-night stand." Patrick sighed.

"We were like that at one time," Ion reminded his friend.

Patrick closed his eyes, and kept his head on Ion's shoulder. "So true, and now we've become those old men we used to make fun of."

Ion rested his cheek on Patrick's curls. "We're still hot. Just more discriminating in our tastes."

"Or pining away for an unrequited love, hmm?"

"Don't start on that, Patrick. You tell me to ask Adrien out all the time, but talk about the flower wishing for the sun. He's way out of my league, and why would he want to go out with a mailroom clerk when he could have any man he wanted?" Ion shook his head, then emptied his glass.

He dislodged Patrick gently before pouring out more wine.

"But he knows your name. That should mean something," Patrick pointed out.

Ion shrugged. "Not really. Adrien knows most of the people who work at the main office. He's just being a good boss. I can't read anything into it."

Patrick started to say something, but Ion held up his hand.

"Come on. Let's go change into some sweats and watch a movie or two. Take our minds off our pathetic dating life."

"Bring out some for me. I don't feel like getting off the couch," Patrick ordered him.

"Fine." Ion shoved to his feet, then went to his bedroom to grab some sweats. He and Patrick were around the same height and weight, so it made sharing clothes easy. "I'm not entirely sure whether these are yours or mine."

He went back into the living room to find Patrick standing by his desk, holding some of the project pages in his hand.

"You shouldn't be looking at those. I don't want you to get in trouble." Ion dropped the clothes on the couch, then strolled over to take the papers away from Patrick.

"Are you serious about these numbers? You've figured out a way to save all those jobs at that company?" Patrick sounded surprised.

"Don't sound shocked." Ion replaced the reports. "I think I did, but that doesn't mean anything. I don't know how I'm going to bring them to Adrien's attention. I mean, it's not like he's going to accept advice from the mail clerk."

Patrick took Ion's hand to lead him back to the couch. He pushed Ion down on it, then sat next to him.

"I'll put them on the conference table for you. Just get them to me before Sunday night. Bellamy's called for a seven o'clock morning meeting for the all the executives. He wants me there this time, so I'll be getting in to the office at six. I'll have more than enough time to put them out."

Ion wasn't sure he should accept Patrick's offer. "You won't get fired, will you? I'm pretty sure it has to be a breach of your confidential clause or something like that."

Patrick shrugged. "I don't really care if it means people won't lose their livelihood. I can find a new job if I need to, but some of those people like your parents won't be able to because of their age."

"Let's finish the wine, and watch some movies. I need to think about it, but if I decide yes, I'll make sure you have them before Sunday night."

Patrick looked like he wanted to keep arguing, but Ion was done discussing it for the night. So he changed quickly, then popped in one of their favorite. He settled back, and soon Patrick joined him. They wrapped the blanket around themselves, then wiggled around until they were both happy.

The movie started, allowing Ion to forget about his plans and proposals.

Chapter Two

Adrien stalked into his office on Monday morning, almost throwing his briefcase through one of the large plate-glass windows making up one of his walls. This past weekend was supposed to have been a relaxing one. He'd planned to take his boat out and sail along the coast. Getting a little alone time in before the big company review, but with the Huntsman Toy debacle hanging over his head, Adrien hadn't been able to justify going.

"Here's your coffee, sir." Patrick walked in, somehow managing to carry Adrien's cup and several folders at once.

Adrien took the cup from Patrick, dredging up a smile. "How many times have I told you not to bring me coffee? You're not my servant, Patrick, though I know there are times you feel I treat you that way. I'm perfectly capable of getting it for myself."

His personal assistant flashed him a bright smile. "It's all right, Mr Bellamy. I was bringing you the files you requested and thought you'd like it."

"You're too good to me, Patrick." He sipped it, made just the way he liked it.

He'd known choosing Patrick as his PA hadn't been a popular choice amongst the executives. Adrien had never hidden his sexual orientation from the people he worked with, so when he'd hired Patrick, most of them thought he'd been swayed by the man's movie star looks. While Patrick was gorgeous, Adrien had made his decision based on Patrick's resume.

"Remember that later," Patrick mumbled as he passed Adrien.

Adrien frowned at the cryptic statement, but he forgot about it as he started glancing through the reports Patrick had brought him. He stood by his desk, fueling up on caffeine while flipping through the pages.

The intercom buzzed, and Patrick's voice came through, "Mr Bellamy, everyone's gathered in the conference room, waiting for you."

"Thanks, Patrick. Let's hope they came up with a solution or I just might fire all of them," he muttered.

He snatched up the files on the Huntsman company before he left his office. Patrick glanced up from his desk as Adrien strolled by.

"Do you want me to take notes?" Patrick asked.

"Actually, yes I do. You need to write down everything they suggest. Maybe among the babble, we can find something worthwhile."

Patrick grabbed his laptop, then trailed Adrien into the room. Adrien glanced around, shocked to see his executives bent over some papers. He set his files on the table at the front of the room.

"All right, everyone. Tell me what you've come up with over the weekend. So I won't want to fire your asses." He propped his hands on his hips as he met each person's gaze.

Sidney cleared his throat.

"What do you want, Sidney?"

"Did you come up with these proposals?" Sidney held up the folder everyone had been looking at.

"What are you talking about?" He picked up the papers, and opened the cover to read the first page.

After the first paragraph, he flopped into his chair to continue reading. As he went through the proposals, excitement started growing in him. This was what he had hoped his people would come up with. The others stayed silent while he went through each suggestion and graph.

When he turned the last page, he leaned back against his chair, and pressed his fingertips together before resting them against his lips. Adrien ran the ideas through his brain, trying to find any flaws. It would take a little time, but with patience, the plans could work.

"All right. Whose idea is this?" Adrien tapped the report in front of him.

Adrien watched as looks of confusion crossed their faces. Sidney shrugged when he glanced at him.

"Are you saying none of you wrote this up?"

They all nodded, looking as confused as Adrien felt.

"Well, if none of you did this, who did? How did they get into the conference room?" He shot to his feet before pacing the length of the room. "It's bloody brilliant, and with a little bit of a monetary investment from us, I think it will work. We won't have to lay off any workers, and we'll be seeing a profit within a year."

A sigh of relief went through the room, and Adrien snorted. Everyone was thrilled that a solution had been found, so Adrien wouldn't be yelling at them about this problem anymore.

"How do we find out who wrote this up? I think they deserve a bonus or something," Sidney spoke up.

Patrick coughed, and Adrien looked over at him. The guilty expression on his assistant's face told Adrien Patrick might know more about the proposal than Adrien thought he did.

"Is there something you want to tell us, Patrick?"

"Umm...I might know who wrote that up." Patrick gestured toward the papers on the table. "If I tell you, you won't fire him or anything, will you? He was trying to help."

"Did you hear what I had to say? Our mysterious author will be getting a big bonus for this, and maybe a promotion because he's been hiding his light under a basket or something." Adrien wanted to grab Patrick and shake the name out of him.

"I have to make a phone call." Patrick dashed from the room.

"What the hell?" One of the executives who didn't like Patrick grumbled. "Where is he going? Does he know or is he just trying to make you think he does?"

"Shut up, Randolph," Adrien ordered. He wasn't a fan of Randolph personally, but the man was good at his job, which was why Adrien hadn't fired him yet. "Let Patrick do what he needs to do."

"While we wait, let's go over the proposal, and see what each of us needs to do to make it happen." Sidney chuckled. "The nice thing is it's all been laid out for us. We just need to start the ball rolling."

Adrien gathered his files, then looked at all of them. "Okay. Sidney, you're in charge of getting this plan up and rolling. I expect a detailed report from each department by the end of the week."

Randolph started to say something, but Adrien held up his hand. "Yes, I expect your people to work on all the other accounts as well. We have four more acquisitions to look at before the board meeting at the end of the month. I need to have the recommendations before then."

Everyone nodded, and Adrien left, knowing he was leaving it in the best hands possible. Sidney's official title was CFO, but he really was Adrien's right hand man. When Adrien took over the company from his father, he'd made sure Sidney came with him.

Patrick was standing by his desk, whispering into his phone. Adrien nodded toward his office as he walked past, and Patrick dipped his head in acknowledgment. As much as Adrien wanted to know the genius behind the Huntsman Toy company proposal, he was willing to wait until Patrick was ready to reveal who the person was.

Adrien sat at the desk, and braced his elbows on the edge. Sighing, he rested his chin on his hand. Relief and excitement coursed through his veins, because he'd been afraid that he'd have to close down the plant, and lay off all those employees.

While making money was the ultimate goal for Bellamy International, Adrien didn't like doing it on the backs of other people. Of course, there were times when he had no other choice except to close down a factory or a plant. Those were the times Adrien would head out on his boat, or hole up in his apartment for a day or two.

His father had often joked about Adrien's soft heart, but Adrien was glad he never became hardened to the problems other people faced. Just because he came from a wealthy family didn't mean he had the right to ignore the working people around him. It was one reason why he'd chosen to work his way up through the company, starting in the mailroom.

A knock brought his head up, and Patrick stood in the doorway. There was someone behind him, but Adrien couldn't see who it was.

"I brought the person who wrote up that proposal, Mr Bellamy." Patrick seemed worried.

"Come on in then." Adrien motioned them in.

Patrick turned slightly, before grabbing the other person's hand. He dragged his companion into the office, and Adrien frowned.

"Ion?"

"Yes, sir. Ion's the one who wrote up those proposals. He spent all weekend doing research and working out scenarios in his head until he couldn't see any other way for it to work. I didn't really look at it, but I encouraged him to show it to you." Patrick shoved Ion in the back to send the man farther into the room.

After standing, Adrien came around his desk to approach Ion slowly. Ion's expression spoke of nerves and worry, but Adrien drank his fill of how amazing Ion looked. While Patrick was movie-star handsome, Ion was almost Olympic god-like.

Ion had unblemished ivory skin and short, dark-brown hair that probably had a tendency to curl if he let it grow long. His brown eyes held an intelligent light. Adrien had noticed Ion the first day he'd started working in the mailroom, and had wanted to ask Ion out right then and there, but he figured the younger man wouldn't be interested in an old guy like him.

"Patrick didn't help me with the proposal. All he did was put them in the conference room. I didn't ask him for any kind of information. Everything that's in there is stuff I found in the public records."

"Patrick, why don't you go get Ion and me some coffee? Or do you want tea or something else?" Adrien suggested, wanting to talk to Ion without Patrick being around.

"Right. I'll bring refreshments right away." Patrick patted Ion on the shoulder before racing out of the office, not waiting for Ion to answer.

Adrien gestured to the couch against one wall. He thought Ion might be more comfortable sitting like that instead of Adrien sitting behind the desk and Ion in a chair. Ion sat, then rubbed his hands on his pants, and Adrien could see how nervous Ion was.

"Don't worry. Patrick isn't in any kind of trouble. In fact, I might give him a bonus for seeing what you had, and ensuring it was brought to my attention." Adrien didn't even think about whether he should do it or not as he reached over to cover Ion's hand with his.

Ion entwined their fingers, holding tight to him. "Are you being honest? This was totally my idea and I don't want him to get in trouble because of it."

"I believe you when you say Patrick didn't tell you anything. He's a lot of things, but he doesn't talk about things he shouldn't. It's one of the things I've come to realize about Patrick. How long have you two been friends?"

Maybe a little small talk would help Ion calm down slightly. Ion swallowed, then seemed to get a hold of himself.

"We've been friends for ten years or so. I met him our junior year in high school. You know how Patrick is, and he hasn't changed much. Some jerks were bullying him, and I stepped in to stop them. Patrick was a new student, so they thought they could get away with teasing him. I'd been going to that school since I hit high school, and they all knew me. We've been friends since then," Ion babbled.

After getting to know Patrick, Adrien never questioned the man's sexuality, and because Ion was Patrick's friend, Adrien hadn't thought about it either. Yet the way Ion clung to his hand, Adrien was sure Ion wouldn't get upset if he were to ask him out.

"Here are your drinks," Patrick said as he hustled back into the office.

Adrien pulled his hand away and put several inches between them. Patrick shot him a quick glance while handing him his coffee, but didn't say anything else.

"I brought you some tea, Ion." Patrick set Ion's cup down on the table. "I have some work to do. If you need anything, just buzz me, Mr Bellamy."

"I will. Thanks, Patrick."

"Certainly." Patrick patted Ion on the shoulder before leaving the office.

Adrien took a sip of his coffee, stalling for a few minutes to collect his thoughts. He knew what he wanted to do on a business level. Ion showed initiative and quite a lot of genius to work out the solution. Adrien was pretty sure Ion would be good for the company in a more challenging capacity than a mailman. Hell, Adrien had been looking for someone to replace Constance who had left for a better paying job out of the country, but he had to find out if Ion was qualified before he offered it.

"Do you have plans to move up from the mailroom?" It was a causal question, but one Adrien thought was important.

Ion nodded. "Yes. I'm a semester away from graduating from Columbia University with an MBA. My goal is to work as a troubleshooter, figuring out situations like the one you had with Huntsman. I like solving problems."

A MBA would be perfect for the job, and being a semester away meant Ion would be finishing it within the next year. He could convince Sidney that hiring Ion for Constance's job would be a good idea. Adrien didn't need anyone's approval to give Ion it, but he would make sure Sidney and Bart, the head of the department Ion would be working in, had a chance to interview him.

"Would you be interested in a new placement here within the company?" Adrien kept his tone light.

Ion grinned. "Yes, sir. I love working here, and that's why I spent all weekend trying to figure out the best way to keep Huntsman Toys up and running. Well that, and because my parents and older brother work there. I'm bound and determined to do what I can to help them keep theirs."

"Is that how you came up with the ideas?" It was one of the things Adrien noticed in the proposal.

"Yes, Mr Bellamy. My brother, Bogdan, is one of the toy engineers at Huntsman, and the ideas he gave me were ones that had been scrapped. He didn't give me anything that was in production since you already had that information. I was pretty sure that the ones he gave me, with a little influx of money, would be profitable." Ion took a deep breath. "I hope that doesn't get him in trouble. I was just using all my resources to find a viable solution."

After reaching out, Adrien set his hand on Ion's knee. He squeezed gently, and Ion's eyes widened. Glancing down, Adrien couldn't help but notice the nice bulge behind the zipper of Ion's pants.

"I promise your brother won't be getting in trouble either. He just might get a raise for seeing the potential in product that had been passed over. I have my financial department going over the numbers, and I think we could probably do what you suggest."

"Really?" Ion wanted to bounce on the couch, but managed to keep control of the happiness inside him. "I know I was asking a lot of him to tell me company stuff, but I also knew that if I could convince you with the proposals, you wouldn't lay anyone off."

Adrien stroked his fingers along the seam on the inside of Ion's pants, trailing them closer to Ion's groin. Ion didn't pull away from him, and Adrien eased closer.

"If I ask you something, will you answer me honestly? Tell me what you think, not what you think I want you to say." Adrien paused for a second, then continued, "And to clear up any question, the offer is not contingent on your answer. I don't work that way."

Ion licked his lips nervously, then nodded. "All right. I'll answer you honestly."

Adrien removed his hand from Ion's, not wanting to influence him. "Will you have dinner with me tonight?"

Shock danced across Ion's face, along with disbelief. "Why would you ask me out? I'm so not in your league."

"I don't care if you're rich and came from a Mayflower family, Ion. I've been interested in you since the first day I met you down in the mailroom. I just wasn't sure you'd be willing to date the boss. I would never want you to think your job here is tied to our dating." Adrien shook his head. "I've dated a few men who worked here, but once we broke it off, I refused to treat them any different than I did before we dated."

"I'd love to go out with you, but I can't tonight. I have class, and I can't skip it." Ion looked and sounded disappointed.

"I understand wanting to further your education. No problem. When would you be able to go?"

If Adrien had something going on that particular night, he'd clear his calendar.

"Would Friday be all right? I don't have class, and we don't have to work the next day."

Adrien couldn't help a little burst of desire at the thought of having a whole weekend with Ion. He hoped their date would go so well, Ion wouldn't want it to end. Maybe that was Ion's hope as well, and why he'd suggested Friday.

"Friday would be wonderful. I could pick you up at your apartment around seven. Would that give you enough time to get home from work?" Adrien sorted through the restaurants he could take Ion to.

He didn't want it to be anything so high-brow, Ion would be uncomfortable eating at, because Ion being unhappy wasn't in Adrien's plan book. Yet he didn't want it to be a greasy spoon where Ion would think Adrien was trying to prove he was just like every other man.

Ion smiled shyly, ducking his head down a little. "Seven would be great. I can get home by then. Do you know where we're going?"

Adrien shrugged. "I have some ideas, but nothing definite. I'll pick one, then let you know how you need to dress. Does that work?"

"Yes." Ion glanced around the office. "What happens now?"

"Now I kiss you because I've been wanting to know what you taste like for a year."

After standing, he took Ion's hands to help Ion to his feet. Adrien slid one of his hands around the back of Ion's head, cradling him like a precious object. He settled his other hand on Ion's hip.

Ion tilted his head, and Adrien pressed their lips together, sweeping his tongue into Ion's mouth. He groaned as Ion's unique flavor danced along his taste buds. Ion melted into his embrace, encircling Adrien's waist and leaning into his body.

Soft and pliable, Adrien thought as he moved his hands to Ion's butt. He flexed his fingers, and Ion moaned, arching into him.

"Mr Bellamy...oh shit! Sorry. Should've locked the fucking door when I left," Patrick said.

The door slammed closed as Adrien and Ion broke apart. He rubbed his thumb over Ion's lower lip, loving how it had plumped slightly from their kiss.

"Patrick won't say a word to anyone," Ion promised.

"I know. Your friend is very secretive when he needs—or wants—to be." Adrien took a deep breath, then stepped farther away from Ion. "Do you have access to your resume?"

Ion blinked at the quick change of subject, but recovered. "Yes."

"Have Patrick print it out for you. I'm going to talk to Mr Richardson and Mr Herner to set up interviews with them for you." Adrien winked. "I'm sure they'll be as impressed with you as I am. Just maybe not for all the same reasons."

Adrien went to his desk before he pushed intercom button. "Patrick, you can come back in here."

"All right, sir."

He could hear the smirk in Patrick's voice, but he chose not to address it. Patrick wouldn't tease him, and he had a feeling Ion could handle Patrick if he had to. Ion rubbed his palms on his pants while he stood in the middle of the office. Adrien sat at his desk, and dialed Sidney's private number.

"Hey man, we're not even halfway through this proposal. Things are looking good, but you did give us until the end of the week." Sidney sounded a little frazzled.

"I remember, and I'm not calling to harass you about that. You'll get it done by then. I have a person I'd like you and Bart to interview for Constance's position. I know Bart's been running a person short, which is causing his people to freak out a little."

Adrien looked up when he heard the door open. Patrick entered then went to bump Ion's shoulder with his. Adrien watched as Patrick leaned over, whispering something in Ion's ear that made Ion blush then shove Patrick away, but he was laughing.

"Who is it?" Sidney hesitated for a moment before continuing, "Did Patrick bring you the guy who wrote this report?"

"Yes, and I'd like you and Bart to meet him. I'm pretty sure you'll see what I see." Adrien tapped his fingers on his desk.

"All right. Let me grab Bart, then give us thirty minutes. We'll meet him in my office."

Sidney usually listened to Adrien when it came to business and employees, though he had his own opinion and would voice it when he felt the need to. Adrien didn't think he would when he met Ion.

"Great. I'll let him know, and I think you're going to be surprised when you meet him."

"What's his name?"

Adrien shook his head, even though Sidney couldn't see him. "I'm not telling. Don't want to bias you against him before he gets his chance."

"Fine. Be that way. Send him over in thirty minutes." Sidney hung up.

"All right, Ion. You and Patrick need to print off two copies of your resume and any references you might have. Then you need to be at Mr Richardson's office in thirty minutes," Adrien informed Ion.

"Oh my God, are you interviewing for Constance's position?" Patrick clapped his hands together, almost squealing in his excitement.

"Yes, he is, but everyone doesn't need to know that, Patrick. You might want to tone down the excitement." He smiled at how happy Patrick looked for Ion.

Patrick mimed zipping his lips, then locking them. Rolling his eyes, Ion grabbed Patrick's arm.

"If you say anything before Mr Bellamy is ready, I'll sic Patrice on you."

The panic in Patrick's eyes had Adrien laughing. "I take it Patrice is quite fierce."

"She's Patrick's twin, and if you think he's hyper, you should meet her. Patrice would wear you out in ten minutes just from talking." Ion's words held a note of truth in them, yet Adrien saw fondness in Ion's smile.

"Patrice is evil. Everyone in my family would tell you that." Patrick crossed himself.

"Thanks so much, Mr Bellamy, for giving me this opportunity."

Ion approached Adrien's desk, holding his hand out. After pushing to his feet, Adrien took Ion's hand to shake. He stroked his thumb over Ion's knuckles, and held on a little longer than he needed.

"You're more than welcome, Ion. You allowed me to save a thousand jobs today, and I can't thank you enough for that. Giving you a promotion is the least I could do for you." Adrien inclined his head, loving how they were both acting like the kiss never happened, and that Patrick hadn't seen it.

"After you're done helping Ion, I need you back here, Patrick. We have some emails to send out, and some meetings to set up."

Ion and Patrick took his statement as a dismissal, and left his office. Adrien wandered over to the windows, staring out over the city.

Adrien hoped that dinner would lead to spending the night together. He had a feeling Ion might be someone he could date for longer than a few weeks. Adrien was looking for a serious relationship. He wasn't interested in one-night stands or weekend flings any more. He was older now, and ready to settle down.

Was Ion going to be the one who stuck around long enough for Adrien to fall in love with?

Chapter Three

Ion paced from one end of his living room to the other. Adrien had contacted him earlier in the day, letting him know they were going to go the Bridge Café.

He wasn't freaked out by Adrien's money or his position running one of the world's biggest companies. None of that was important. Ion was nervous because Adrien was so good-looking, that Ion didn't understand why the man would want to go out with him.

His phone rang, and he checked the screen. Answering it, he said, "I really don't want to talk right now."

"Oh Ion, I wasn't calling to give you a hard time. I just wanted to tell you to enjoy yourself. Let whatever happens happen." Patrick sounded serious about the whole thing.

"I plan on it. I have to admit, Patrick, I'm really hoping this goes well." Ion flopped onto the couch, but almost immediately jumped back onto his feet.

"Of course, you do. Adrien Bellamy is one of the most eligible bachelors in the world, and he's a nice guy, which is overkill in my opinion. No man should be that rich, gorgeous, and be a good person as well." Patrick huffed in annoyance.

Ion laughed. "True, but you know me. I don't care about money and looks. Sure, it helps to have those. Ultimately though, it's more important to be a nice person."

Patrick sighed, and Ion could picture him shaking his head. "I love you, honey. I truly do, but some days I don't understand where you're coming from."

"I know you feel the same way I do, so don't act all shallow and everything. I've seen how you look at Mr Richardson. He's handsome, rich, and a nice guy." Ion teased.

Patrick squeaked, than started to mutter, "You better not tell anyone about my unrequited love for Richardson. The man is straighter than a ruler. There's no way I have a chance with him, but I don't want anyone pitying me because of it."

After chuckling, Ion tried to reassure his friend. "You know I'm not going to say a word to anyone, Patrick. Your secret is safe with me."

A knock sounded on the door, and Ion inhaled sharply.

"Adrien must be there," Patrick said. "We'll have lunch on Monday, so you can tell me all about it. I better not hear from you until then."

"Love you, too," Ion said before hanging up.

He rubbed his sweaty palms on his pants, then checked his reflection in the mirror by the door one last time. Ion opened the door with a smile, but his jaw almost hit the floor when he saw Adrien standing in front of him.

Seeing the man in suits all day at the office had told Ion Adrien had a sense of style and loved tailored clothing. Obviously Adrien stepped it up a notch when it came to going out on a date. The dark blue silky dress shirt he wore clung to him like a second skin. Adrien's black slacks emphasized his muscled thighs, and Ion couldn't wait to see what it did to Adrien's backside. The man oozed sex and charisma from every pore.

"I'm going to have to fight everyone off you with a stick," Ion mumbled.

After Adrien strolled in, he swept Ion into his arms then kissed him. Ion forgot every worry and nervous thought he might have had as soon as Adrien's lips touched his. He buried his fingers in Adrien's hair, holding tight while Adrien overwhelmed him.

The only thought in Ion's brain was how soon could he get Adrien into his bed, and was he hungry enough for food to leave his apartment. It wasn't until his lungs burnt from lack of oxygen that he decided to take a step back.

Adrien didn't let him break their embrace. He rested his forehead against Ion's, and they slowed their breathing together.

"I want you, Ion. More than I've ever wanted another man before, and that's saying something."

A small jolt of jealousy hit Ion, but he knew it was stupid to feel that way. Adrien was a mature male with money and power. Of course, he was going to have a lot of lovers before Ion. A tiny voice in Ion's head said that he wouldn't be having any other lovers after Ion if Ion had any say in it.

"I want you as well, Adrien."

Adrien took a step back, leaving his hands at Ion's hips. "But I want us to have dinner together, and get to know each other better before we jump into bed. I think we're looking for the same thing here, and it isn't a quick roll in the hay."

Ion shook his head. "It might seem odd, because I'm not that old, but I'm tired of the club scene and hookups. Maybe it's because I have big plans for myself, and it doesn't seem like a lot of the guys I run into are interested in that."

"Maybe you just needed a mature man to see the possibilities with you." Adrien dove in for a quick peck. "We should be going. Our reservations are for eight o'clock and we don't want to be late."

Ion grabbed his jacket, and his keys. He checked his back pocket to make sure he had his wallet. After locking the door behind him, he followed Adrien to the elevator, getting a chance to see that his assumption was right. The slacks Adrien wore made his ass look perfect.

There was no one on the elevator, so Ion crowded close to Adrien, sliding his hand around behind Adrien to grab his butt cheek. Adrien simply grinned at him while pushing back into Ion's hand.

"You better be careful what you start, Ion, because we might not make it to dinner if you keep it up."

Ion shrugged. "Maybe dinner's overrated."

Adrien laughed. "It might be, but humor me on this. I'd really like you to know it's more than just sex between us. I think we have the possibility of something marvelous."

After giving Adrien one last squeeze, Ion removed his hand from Adrien's cheek to entwine their fingers together. "All right. Tonight, we'll do it your way."

"Thank you."

Ion loved walking out onto the sidewalk, holding hands with Adrien. Both women and men checked them out, and Ion grinned as Adrien hailed a cab for them. When the vehicle stopped at the curb, Ion opened the back door and Adrien slid in. After he joined Adrien, his date told the cabbie where they were going.

They settled back to enjoy the ride across town.

* * * *

"Dinner was great. Thanks so much," Ion said as he and Adrien left The Bridge Café.

"It was good. This is the first time I've been there. I've heard good reviews on it." Adrien flagged down a taxi. Before one arrived, he turned to Ion. "Where would you like to go?"

Ion frowned. "Go? What do you mean?"

"Would you rather go to my place? Or do you want to go back to your apartment?" Adrien smiled. "Either way is fine with me, as long as you understand that we will be ending up in bed wherever we go."

A shiver cascaded through Ion at the thought of having sex with Adrien. How many fantasies of them together had he had since starting at Bellamy International? All of them would be coming true in minutes.

"How about we go to your place? I can always run home tomorrow, and get clean clothes." Ion really was hoping Adrien would agree to let him spend the entire weekend.

"Sounds like a great idea."

A cab stopped, and Adrien held the door open for Ion. After he slid in, Adrien joined him in the back seat. Adrien gave the driver his address, then wrapped his arm around Ion.

Ion rested his head on Adrien's shoulder, comfortable with not saying anything at the moment. He put his hand on his soon-to-be lover's thigh, slowly trailing his fingers up and down the firm muscle. Each time he got close to the nice-sized bulge behind Adrien's zipper, but didn't actually touch it.

He grinned when Adrien covered his hand, putting a halt to his teasing.

"I don't want to go off before we even get naked, Ion," Adrien murmured close to his ear. "The first time I come with you, I want to be inside you."

Ion felt his hole clench at the comment. He whimpered softly, and Adrien chuckled.

"If I can't tease you, you can't do it either," Ion complained.

"Hmm…honey, just wait until I get you back to my place, I'll show you how much I can tease." Adrien nuzzled the side of Ion's face.

Ion's cock stiffened, and he shifted slightly, trying to find room in his pants. He stared out of the window, watching traffic go by as they traveled through the city to Adrien's apartment.

He stood on the sidewalk, waiting for Adrien to pay the driver. Staring up at the building, Ion couldn't believe how modern and beautiful the place was. He glanced over at Adrien when the man came up next to him.

"This is a nice place," he said.

Adrien gestured toward the door. "Let's go up. My apartment is the top floor."

The doorman greeted them as they entered. "Did you have a good dinner, Mr Bellamy?"

"I did, Guilleme. This is Ion. I'm sure you'll be seeing a lot of him from now on."

"Nice to meet you, Mr Ion." Smiling, Guilleme nodded at Ion.

"Nice meeting you as well." Ion was stunned by Adrien's introduction of him. It made him feel good to know Adrien really did mean what he'd said back in Ion's apartment about this being a serious relationship.

As they continued on to the elevator, Ion looked around at the glass and steel walls that were very architectural beautiful.

"Do you own this building?" He had to ask.

Adrien pressed the call button. "Yes. Bellamy International bought the place three years ago. I took over the top floor and had it renovated into one apartment instead of three. I have a house in New Haven where my boat is moored."

Ion stepped into the elevator when it arrived. Adrien followed, then put a key into the panel.

"You have a boat?"

"Yes. I bought it when I became CEO and President. I'd seen how my dad would come home full of stress and annoyed, and he ended with heart problems. I didn't want to be like him."

The doors closed, shutting them into a world all their own. Adrien encircled Ion's waist, pulling him near. Ion snuggled close, enjoying the tender moments as much as he knew he would the sex.

"I'd always liked sailing, so I decided I was going to buy a boat and sail as often as I could to help relieve the stress. It's been working so far. I've been in charge of the company for seven years now, and I'm still healthy." Adrien laughed. "Of course, it helps that I don't smoke, and don't drink to excess like Father did. Also, I work out at least four times a week, if not more."

"Is that why you had a gym put in at the main headquarters?"

Ion took advantage of the gym while he was at work. He didn't often get a chance to go afterwards, because of classes.

When the elevator slowed then dinged, Ion stepped back slightly, but didn't break the embrace. He walked into the foyer of Adrien's apartment. It had hard wood floors, and Ion had a feeling those floors went through the entire space.

"I put the gym in because I want everyone to have a chance to get healthy. I'm not forcing anyone to do it." Adrien drew Ion farther into the apartment. "Why don't you sit and I'll pour us some wine? What do you like—red or white?"

"Whatever you're going to have is fine."

He sat on the couch, staring all around him. While the furnishings spoke of money and luxury, they weren't so outrageous that Ion wouldn't feel like he could put his feet up on the furniture. In fact, he kicked off his shoes, then curled his feet under him as he sat on the couch.

"I love your place," he called out.

Adrien strolled back in, holding two glasses. "Thank you. My mother helped me decorate after the renovations, though I had to rein her in at times. She really wanted to put in a ton of antiques and leather. I kept telling her that isn't who I am. I'm not about flashing my money around."

Ion took his glass from Adrien then sipped. Adrien sat next to him, and Ion took a moment to soak in the warmth emanating from him. He leaned into Adrien's side, relaxing as he drank.

"Would you like to see my bedroom?"

Chuckling, Ion set his glass on the coffee table, then turned to look at Adrien. "That's really smooth. Do you get many men with that?"

"I haven't done bad." Adrien smirked as he stood, offering his hand to Ion. "We both knew it was going to end up there any way."

"True." Ion let Adrien pull him to his feet. "You must think I'm easy."

"No more easy than I am. I'm not a playboy anymore. I was when I was in my twenties. Hell, being the only son of one of the richest men in America gave me a big head."

Ion reached down to press his palm against Adrien's fabric-covered cock. "I do see what you mean about a big head."

Growling, Adrien yanked him forward, then crushed their lips together. Ion loved the forceful way Adrien manhandled him. He admitted he was more of a bottom than a top, though he didn't mind fucking a guy once in a while.

He melted against Adrien, encircling his waist to press as close as he could get with clothes on. Adrien slid his hands down Ion's back to grab his ass. Ion moaned, rocking his hips into Adrien's.

Opening his mouth, he allowed Adrien to sweep in, teasing and tasting every inch of his mouth. He sucked on Adrien's tongue, doing all he could to turn Adrien on until the man's control broke.

Adrien tore his lips away from Ion's, then bent slightly to throw Ion over his shoulder. Ion chuckled as Adrien carried him down the hall toward his bedroom, or at least Ion hoped it was the bedroom.

"Sorry. Got closer than I thought."

"Doors?"

Ion heard the click of a doorknob, then Adrien stepped through into another large room. The doors he was talking about were the enormous mahogany double ones leading into Adrien's bedroom. He grunted when Adrien dropped him onto a soft mattress.

"I need you to get naked as soon as possible," Adrien ordered him.

Struggling to sit up, Ion glanced over at him, and what he saw made his mouth water. Adrien already had his shirt off, and was working on his pants. A large expanse of tanned skin covering a muscular chest with a light dusting of hair had been revealed, and all Ion wanted was to run his hands all over that flesh.

He crawled across the bed in Adrien's direction, reaching out to trail his hands over Adrien's chest, down his washboard stomach to stuff them under Adrien's pants. Ion wrapped his hand around Adrien's cock, stroking it hard and fast.

"God, your hand feels amazing. I bet your mouth would feel even better." Adrien slid his hand around the back of Ion's head, encouraging him to move closer.

Oh, he was more than willing to get his lips around the thick length between Adrien's thighs. He scooted to the edge of the bed and braced one hand on Adrien's knee while keeping his grip on Adrien's erection.

After opening his mouth wide, Ion swallowed Adrien down until he hit the back of Ion's throat.

"Holy shit! I can't believe you can take the whole thing." Adrien tightened his hold on Ion's head, then tugged on his hair to get him to move.

Ion started bobbing up and down, letting his spit drip down to cover the entire length of Adrien's cock. He used his hand to pump as he sucked. Adrien thrust in time with him, and Ion loved how his jaw was stretched by Adrien's girth. He couldn't wait to get Adrien's dick in his ass.

After doing everything he could think of with his mouth and tongue, Ion reached down to fondle Adrien's balls, rolling them in his palms.

"Jesus, Ion. I want to fuck you so bad," Adrien confessed.

Ion glanced up to meet Adrien's heated gaze. He quirked his eyebrow, and Adrien snarled. He held Ion's head still, then slowly slid out. Ion whimpered when Adrien pushed him onto his back.

Adrien ripped Ion's shirt open, and the buttons flew across the room. "I'll buy you a new one."

"I don't care. Just get me naked. I want you inside me now." Ion lifted his hips off the comforter, giving Adrien as much access to Ion's pants as he wanted.

Swearing while he fumbled with the buttons on Ion's pants, Adrien tore the zipper open, and Ion groaned at the strength Adrien displayed. He was quickly stripped of the rest of his clothes. He spread his legs, offering himself.

"Shit." Adrien turned away to dig through the drawer of the nightstand next to the bed. "Thank God."

Ion looked to see Adrien holding a bottle of lube and a strip of condoms. The triumphant grin on Adrien's face made Ion smile. His heart cracked a bit, and Ion found himself falling a little in love.

Adrien crawled on to the bed before wedging between Ion's legs. Ion propped himself up on his elbows so he could watch what he was doing. He bit his lip when Adrien licked a line from the base of Ion's cock to the head. Adrien slipped the tip into his mouth, playing with the slit until Ion tried to thrust his erection further in.

He barely noticed the pop of the lube bottle, but he hissed as Adrien rubbed the cool slick between Ion's cheeks. Ion pulled his legs up to his chest, giving Adrien room to move.

"Please," he begged, wishing for more than just Adrien touching him. "I need you in me."

"We have to stretch you first. I don't want to hurt you, Ion, no matter how much I wish to fuck you."

Ion slid another inch deeper in love, and he stretched his free hand out to run his fingers through Adrien's hair. "I'm thrilled that you care enough to make sure I'm not in pain, but I really want you, and I'm not a patient person."

"All right," Adrien agreed.

After pouring some more lube on his fingers, Adrien pressed one in, and Ion moaned, letting his head fall back. He rocked the best he could, trying to fuck himself on it. Then Adrien added two more fingers, filling Ion, but not as much as he wanted.

Adrien stroked in and out, somehow managing to hit Ion's gland each time. Ion cried out as pleasure raced along his nerves, pooling in his groin. His cock stiffened, rising from its nest of curls, catching Adrien's attention.

"Oh God," Ion shouted as Adrien swallowed his length down. He undulated between Adrien's mouth and his fingers.

His climax burst inside him, and he spilled his cum into Adrien's mouth. Ion trembled and panted as his orgasm waved through him. Adrien kept sucking until Ion stopped moving, then he licked Ion clean.

When the touch of Adrien's tongue got to be too much, Ion pushed on his shoulder.

Adrien let him slip out, then sat back on his heels. Ion lay limp while he watched Adrien rip open the packet to get the rubber out. Adrien shuddered as he rolled the condom along the length of his cock. He squirted some lube on his erection and smeared to coat it.

Ion caught both his knees, bringing them up and to the sides, exposing his hole to Adrien.

"So beautiful," Adrien murmured, running his hands over Ion's ass before positioning his length at Ion's opening.

"So are you," Ion whispered, then he held his breath as Adrien sank into him.

There was some burning because Adrien was thicker than Ion's other lovers had been, and he hadn't let Adrien stretch him enough. Ion breathed out, trying to relax and allow Adrien thrust as deep inside as he could.

This was the fullness Ion had been looking for, and when Adrien bottomed out, he wrapped his legs around Adrien's waist. Adrien braced his hands on each side of Ion's head, staring down into his eyes.

"Ready for me to move?"

Ion could see Adrien's arms tremble with the man's need to start riding him. Ion smiled up at Adrien, and nodded.

"Yes. I want to feel you for days. Take me as hard as you can, Adrien."

"Thank God."

Adrien drove into Ion, each stroke faster than the first. Ion shoved his hands against the headboard to keep from banging his head against it. It also gave him leverage to push back, causing their bodies to slam together hard enough to force his breath from his lungs.

Grunts and sounds of skin on skin filled the air, and Ion did everything he could to encourage Adrien to fuck him. Adrien's hot breath bathed Ion's face as he reamed Ion's ass.

"Oh God, Ion," Adrien yelled as Ion clenched his inner muscles around Adrien's length.

"That's it. I can feel you so hard and deep inside me. Whenever I sit the rest of this weekend, I'll remember what you did to me. I want it. I want you. Hell, I need you. Please."

Adrien slammed into him, then froze. Adrien jerked and swore as his climax hit him. Ion continued the internal massage of Adrien's cock, trying to get every drop of cum from him.

Finally Adrien collapsed to the side, and Ion moaned as he slid out of him. They both lay on the bed, panting and working on calming their heartbeats. Adrien took the condom off carefully, then wrapped it in tissue before tossing it in the wastebasket by the bed.

Ion allowed Adrien to shift and move him until he was under the comforter and sheets. After Adrien rejoined him, Ion rolled over to rest his head on Adrien's shoulder. Ion trailed his fingers up and down Adrien's chest.

"That was amazing," he murmured, not sure he could climb out of bed if he tried.

"It was the best sex I've ever had." Adrien covered Ion's hand with his.

Ion snorted. "You don't have to say that to make me feel better."

Adrien shook his head. "No, I really mean it. I wouldn't say if I didn't feel that it was true. There's a connection between us, and I'd like to see where it leads us."

Ion took a deep breath. He could either act like he has no idea what Adrien was talking about or he could let him know he wasn't the only one who felt that way.

"I'm in the same boat as you. Falling for you could be the easiest thing I'll ever do."

"I'm glad."

"So am I."

Silence blanketed the room as he soaked in the possibilities of their blossoming relationship.

Chapter Four

Stretching, Ion rolled onto his side and jumped when his arm made contact with another warm body. He opened his eyes to see Adrien lying next to him. *Oh right! Second night together, and some of the best sex I've ever had.*

Adrien had asked him out to dinner again for Saturday night, and Ion had accepted. They'd gone to another nice, but not too high-class restaurant, then came back to Adrien's place for another round of sex. It was crazy how easily they got along. He'd never met a guy he could talk to like he did Adrien.

They'd talked about the possibility of their relationship becoming serious the first night they slept together, but Ion wasn't convinced that Adrien would want to keep him around for long. Because really? What did Ion have to offer a man like Adrien?

Oh, Ion wasn't ashamed of where he came from and the life he had, but he knew that there would be a lot of people who might think he was with Adrien simply because of his money, and the possibility of what he could do for Ion's career.

He thought about the offer Mr Richardson had made him on Friday. Working for Mr Herner as a problem solver at Bellamy International was a dream job for him, and he was willing to be on probation until he graduated. He'd said yes, and Mr Herner had said they would talk to Adrien on Monday, so Ion wasn't going to mention it unless Adrien did.

"You're thinking too hard for a Sunday morning."

Ion refocused on the man in bed with him. Adrien studied him with his bright blue eyes, almost like he knew what Ion was thinking. But instead of saying anything, Adrien slid his hand around to cup the back of Ion's head, then drew him down to him.

Their lips met, and he let go of all the thoughts in his head. Why dwell on that stuff when he had one of the world's sexiest men in his bed? Opening his mouth allowed Adrien to sweep his tongue in, and Ion moaned.

His cock twitched as he pressed as close to Adrien as he could without climbing under his skin. When Adrien encircled his waist with his other arm, Ion went as Adrien encouraged him to lie on top of him. Ion ground their groins together, loving the feel of his lover's erection rubbing against his.

Adrien bit his bottom lip, then sucked on it to ease the sting. Ion shuddered as he continued moving, slowly becoming lost in the kiss and embrace. He'd had a bit of a dry spell in the 'having sex' part of his life, mostly because he'd been working hard to finish up his degree.

Oh he'd had his fair share of one-night stands and weekend lovers, but lately he'd just been too tired to go out after work and school. A pinch brought his mind back to the hot man in his bed.

"You weren't here with me," Adrien complained when Ion glared at him.

"How could I not be when you're so fucking hot?" Ion exhaled when Adrien flexed, and he suddenly found himself on his back with Adrien over top of him.

He bit his lip when his cock slid over Adrien's erection. *Oh my God, how can this man be so beautiful and smart as well? It's so not fair.* As they moved together, his excitement built. He wanted Adrien again, and he didn't want to wait.

Scrambling through the sheets, he found the lube. Ion thrust it in Adrien's face. "Now. I want you inside me as soon as you can. Don't waste too much time on getting me ready."

"I don't want to hurt you," Adrien protested, though he reared back on his heels to pop the lid then squirted some on his fingers.

He spread his legs. He didn't care how vulnerable it made him or how slutty it might have looked. All he cared about was making sure Adrien got inside him as quick as possible.

"Don't worry about me. I just want you to fuck me," he demanded.

Adrien chuckled, but did as Ion ordered. He rubbed his fingertips over Ion's opening before easing one of them into the tight ring of muscle. Ion bit his bottom lip as the slight burn rose in him. Breathing deep, he relaxed, pushing out to help Adrien stretch him.

He didn't let his lover take long. After only a few minutes, he let go of one of his knees to snatch a condom from where they'd ended up. He tossed it to Adrien. "Put it on. I want you now. Please."

After rolling over onto his hands and knees, Ion buried his face in the pillow while shoving his ass into

Adrien's face. He yelped when a stinging slap landed on his butt cheek. He glared over his shoulder at Adrien.

"What was that for?"

Adrien shrugged and grinned. "Just felt like it. You offered it up so pretty like."

He shook it. "I'd rather you fucked it, not slap it."

"All right."

Ion sighed as Adrien took his place between Ion's legs. He felt Adrien position his cock at his anus, then thrust in. He groaned into the pillow as Adrien filled him, and Ion loved how big Adrien's dick felt.

There was a pause once Adrien was buried all the way in like he was waiting for Ion to adjust. Ion clenched his passage around Adrien's shaft, then pushed back a little, and his lover took the hint.

Adrien started slow, stroking in and out while gripping Ion's hips. There were going to be bruises there, but Ion didn't care. Firstly, it wasn't like anyone would be able to see them, and secondly, he liked the idea of seeing and feeling Adrien a day or two after their weekend together.

He tilted his hips, trying for a different angle. It caused Adrien to go deeper, then as he pulled out, he bumped Ion's gland. Shaking, Ion moaned and pushed back, wanting more.

"Christ, your ass is so tight, Ion. I love it." Adrien grunted as he began slamming into Ion.

"Holy shit!" Ion moved in unison, doing his best to drive Adrien over the edge.

Ion cried out as Adrien reached to wrap his hand around Ion's length. With each thrust, Adrien slid Ion's flesh through the tunnel of his fingers, and Ion's climax built until he couldn't take it anymore. Pleasure danced along his spine as he shouted, then coated Adrien's hand and the sheet beneath his with his cum.

When his climax caused him to clench his passage tighter than before, Adrien shoved in deep, then froze when he joined Ion in the abyss of lust. Ion turned his head in enough time not to smother in the pillow when they collapsed into a heap together.

Their arms and legs were tangled, and Ion listened to Adrien's heartbeat slow down. He winced when Adrien slid from him. His lover climbed out before he headed for the bathroom. He heard water running, and contemplated getting up to change the sheets on the bed, but he just couldn't work up the energy.

Adrien smiled down at him when he returned. "Are you going to sleep in the wet spot or do we change the bedding?"

Sighing, he got up. "I'll go wash up, then we can change them."

When he got back, Adrien had stripped the mattress and had retrieved the clean set of sheets.

"I didn't think you knew how to make a bed," Ion teased as they began to put it back in order.

"I might be rich, but I can do things for myself. I don't expect my housekeeper to pick up after me. I mean, sure, she takes care of my laundry sometimes because I don't have time for that." Adrien pursed his lips as he paused.

Ion raised his eyebrows. A housekeeper? And the man didn't expect her to pick up after him? "That's big of you. I'm sure she appreciates how much you do around your place."

Adrien reached across the bed and smacked Ion in the arm. "You know what I mean."

He did get it, though he still didn't quite grasp the having enough money for a housekeeper part of things. "Sure."

"When I was little, we had servants to clean up after us, but once I went away to boarding school and college, I didn't have anyone. I had to learn how to do it for myself. Most of the time now, I do, but sometimes I'm too busy and she comes in to clean." Adrien tucked in one corner of the sheet. "I don't eat in a lot either. I work late at the office because some of the businesses we're in charge of are on the other side of the world."

Once the bed were changed, they climbed back in, and Ion snuggled close to Adrien, loving how warm he was. Also, the sheets were the softest he'd ever felt. He ran his fingers over them.

"What kind of count are these?" Curiosity made him ask.

Adrien's shrug caused Ion's head to move. "I don't know. My decorator bought them for me. I can ask her."

Ion shook his head. "No, I was just being nosy."

"Do you have plans for today?" Adrien dragged his fingers up and down Ion's back, drawing goose bumps.

"I have to go to my parents' for dinner tonight. It's mandatory. If I don't show up, I had better be sick or out of town." Ion smiled. "It's really the only thing my mother expects of us."

"Can you bring friends?"

Pushing away from Adrien, Ion tried to figure out where he was going with that question. "Sure. Mom makes a ton of food, so one more won't really make that big of difference."

"Do you think I could join you?"

"Today?"

Adrien nodded at the same time that Ion shook his head.

"I don't think that's a good idea. We've just started dating, and I don't want to frighten you off." Ion took Adrien's hand. "My parents can be a little overwhelming. Hell, my whole family can try the patience of a saint."

"Just wait until you meet my parents. There isn't anyone more trying than my mother. My father can't be bothered by anything except his racing now that he retired from the business." Adrien squeezed Ion's hand. "I'm also the CEO of a Fortune 100 company. Do you seriously think your parents will scare me?"

He wasn't sure about that, especially his mother, but he wasn't about to tell Adrien that. No man wanted to be thought of as being cowed by a four-foot-eleven-inch-tall woman.

"Maybe not, but I'm not sure we're ready to be meeting the parents yet. If we're together a month from now, then we can think about you coming to dinner with me."

Adrien didn't look happy about Ion pushing the parent meeting further out, but Ion knew better than to bring Adrien to his childhood home without warning his mother that he was coming. If it was just family, she didn't worry about how the place looked, but if he was bringing strangers, she would need to spend all day cleaning.

Once his family discovered that he was dating his boss, and the man who owned the toy company they worked for, things would be even stranger. Of course, the other issue would be simply that Adrien was a man, not a nice respectable girl.

"I guess you're right, though I do plan on us still dating in a month and longer." Adrien sounded so positive that Ion didn't have the heart to doubt him.

"I'm more than happy to have that come true. But until then, what do you want to do until I have to go?"

"Hold you for a little while longer, then go to brunch. Maybe hit one of the museums afterwards." Adrien tugged on his hand to bring him back into his embrace. "You don't have to do homework or anything like that?"

Ion cuddled close. "I'll use it as an excuse to get out of having to stay at my parents for too long."

Adrien's chuckle warmed Ion's heart. "I try to find any excuse I can to get out of having dinner with my parents. But there are times when Mother demands my presence, and I can't say no. I tried that once when I first moved out. Worst idea of my life. She called me every day telling me what a terrible son I was, and how could I treat my mother like that. I wanted to tell her that she might have given birth to me, but she didn't raise me. That's what my nanny was for. But I was smart and kept my mouth shut."

"Did you give in?" Ion grinned, having listened to that same type of guilt trip from his mother as well.

"Yes. I couldn't take it anymore, so now when she tells me to come for dinner, I show up."

He tucked the blankets around them as they settled in for a little more rest. Ion couldn't believe how comfortable he felt just hanging with Adrien, even though they'd only spent two nights together so far. Hopefully after spending the day with him, Ion would be able to let himself start to seriously consider falling for him

* * * *

"Did you hear the news, Ion?" his mother asked as he wandered into his childhood home that evening. She wrapped her thin arms around his waist, then crushed him to her. He hugged her back, breathing in the familiar scent of her White Diamonds perfume.

"What news, Mama? I just got here."

She waited while he removed his coat before hanging it up. Once he was ready to go, she grabbed his hand to drag him through the house to the kitchen. Olive was cutting up some vegetables, and Ion went to brush a kiss over her cheek.

"You're looking gorgeous as ever," he said before he went to get a beer out of the fridge.

"Thank you, Ion." She gave him a quick smile, but he saw the tiredness around her eyes and the grooves at the sides of her mouth.

Things had been tough for his family in the last year or two. He knew that the sale of the company to Bellamy had caused them all to worry about their jobs.

Bogdan and Olive had kids to worry about. House payments, bills and the future college expenses weighed heavily on their minds. So he wasn't surprised to see Olive looking exhausted. Ion just hoped that the news that the company wasn't closing would help lift all of their spirits.

"The news, Ion. Did you hear it?" Mama gestured and the way she waved her hands made Ion happy she wasn't holding a knife.

"No, Mama. I haven't heard anything. I was busy all day." He wasn't about to tell her that he'd spent the morning in Adrien's bed, and the afternoon wandering around the Museum of Modern Art with him.

"The company isn't closing. We're not going to lose our jobs, and neither is Bogdan. Isn't that wonderful?" Her smile brightened her wrinkled face, and her joy brought a grin to Ion's as well.

"That's wonderful, Mama." He hugged her again. "How did you learn about it?"

"Maria, who is the secretary for the president of Huntsman, called to tell us." She grimaced. "She probably wasn't supposed to let us know, but she said she couldn't sit on the information all weekend. She knew how worried we all were about it."

Ion wished he could've called his parents the minute he knew the company wouldn't be shut down, but he didn't want to explain how he knew. He didn't want his parents to know it was his proposal that saved their jobs.

Bogdan wandered into the kitchen. Smiling, he slapped Ion on the shoulder. "Good to see you, little brother. Mama telling you?"

He gave his brother a quick one-armed hug. "Yes, she is. It's great. I'm glad to know none of you will have to be looking for new jobs in a month."

"So am I." Bogdan shot him a questioning glance. "Pretty amazing that the company found a way to keep Huntsman open without laying anyone off."

"That's why they make the big bucks, brother. I'm just a mail clerk, so I don't have access to that kind of information." Ion shrugged, though he could tell from the look he got from Bogdan, his brother would be cornering him later on when the others weren't around. "Where's Pops?"

"He's watching the game. Why don't you go in and talk with him? Olive and I will finish up getting dinner on the table." Mama made a shooing motion to get him and his brother out of the room.

After wandering a little ways down the hallway toward the front room, Bogdan pulled Ion to a halt. "Are you the reason why we get to keep our jobs?"

"You can't tell anyone, Bogdan. The people at work know I wrote up the proposal, but you can't tell Mama and Pops. I don't want them to know yet, though I'm sure they'll find out soon enough."

His brother studied him for a moment. "What happened? There's something different about you."

"I got a promotion at work. I'm now going to be a troubleshooter at Bellamy International, or at least, I'll be a junior one until I get my degree." Ion did a little jig in the middle of the corridor.

"Troubleshooter? Is that what you did with the Huntsman problem? You found a solution, and they'll have you find other solutions to other problems?" Bogdan frowned as he tried to figure out what exactly Ion wanted to do.

"Right. It'll mean more money too, so I'll be able to pay off my student loans quicker." Just that knowledge lifted a weight off his shoulder. He'd never asked his parents for anything. They'd had such a difficult time sending Bogdan to college and had to mortgage their house they were still paying off. Ion didn't want to make it harder for them, so he'd paid for all his classes on his own.

Bogdan hugged him. "That's great news, Ion. Are you going to tell them tonight? It might get them to stop telling you to get a real job."

"No. I'm going to let them be happy about keeping their jobs. I can tell them some other day." He glanced over his shoulder at the kitchen, then back at Bogdan. "I met someone, too. We had a date and spent some time together. He wanted to come tonight, but I told him we should wait until we've been together for a while. I don't want Mama scaring him off."

"Oh Ion, I'm not sure bringing a guy to meet them would be good, no matter how long you've been seeing each other." Bogdan frowned. "They are old-fashioned, and I don't think they'll ever truly change. They love you, Ion, but you being gay is wrong to them."

Ion nodded. "I know that, but I'm not going to hide who I am, and I refuse to hide the man I love. I want them to meet him, and if they can't find a way to welcome him into the family, then I won't be coming for family dinners anymore."

"You need to give them time." His brother started toward the front room. "You can't expect them to just accept it all without hoping you'll change."

"Why shouldn't I expect that? I'm not going to, and they've had years to get used to it. They should know that I'd meet some guy and fall in love with him. I'd want them to meet him and welcome him into the family like they did Olive." Ion wanted to continue arguing, but they'd walked into the front room where his dad sat watching the baseball game.

"Hey, Pops, congratulations on keeping your job." Ion clapped him on the shoulder before taking a seat on the couch next to his father's chair.

His father sniffed, but Ion could see that he was pleased. Pops wasn't much of a talker and Ion had learnt how to tell his moods by the tilt of his mouth. He glanced over at the TV.

"See the Sox are beating the Yankees again," he commented.

"Yep. Yankees are a bunch of deadbeats." Pops slapped his thigh in disgust before shooting Ion a glance. "Work going well for you? Still a mailman?"

Ion stopped himself from rolling his eyes. His father always asked him that. "Work's good, Pops. I'm still working at Bellamy International in the mail room."

That part was true. He wasn't scheduled to start his new job until the middle of the week.

"I don't understand why you go to college and spend all that money on those classes just so you can work as a mailman for a company. It makes no sense to me." Pops shook his head.

"I'm not going to be working in the mail room for long. Once I get my degree, I'll find a job better suited for my education. I don't understand why we have to have this conversation every time. At least I have a job, and can pay my own way. Shouldn't you be happy about that?" He gestured to the ceiling above him. "I could still be living here, sponging off you and Mama."

His father didn't look at him, but he grunted, and Ion took it as agreement. He knew it wouldn't stop Pops from making comments about his job, but Ion hoped that his promotion would change things once he told him.

His phone vibrated in his pocket, and he pulled it out to check the screen. It was a text from Adrien.

Hope you're having a good time with the family.

After running his finger across the screen, he got the text part up and typed in *It's been great. They're happy about keeping their jobs.*

Did you tell them you did it?

Pops scowled at him, letting him know that he didn't appreciate Ion texting while in the middle of their conversation. Even though they weren't really talking about anything.

I don't plan on doing that. They don't need to know I did it.

Why not? You saved their jobs. Shouldn't you want the recognition?

Ion snorted softly. He didn't care since he didn't do it just for them. He'd wanted to help out his brother and all the other people who worked at the toy company.

Don't need the recognition as long as they keep their jobs. Miss you.

He hit send, then wished he could take that back. Was it too soon to start doing the 'miss you' thing? Especially when they'd only been apart for a couple of hours in all. He didn't want to be needy or clingy.

Miss you too. Had fun this afternoon. Definitely want to do it again.

"Dinner's ready, boys. Come on," Mama shouted from the dining room.

Have to go. Dinner's ready. See you tomorrow.

Ion sent the text, then stuffed his phone back in his pocket. It vibrated, but he didn't pull it out. His mama didn't like phones at the table and he tried to respect that.

Chapter Five

Adrien looked up as Sidney strode into his office. He nodded toward the chair in front of his desk, letting his friend know he would be with him in a minute. After going through Ion's proposal, Adrien couldn't see anything wrong with it, and he wanted to put it into action as soon as his people could.

"Will it hold up?" Sidney gestured at the file.

"Yes." Adrien sent off his approval to Diggs, the man he'd put in charge of the Huntsman Toys recovery. "Diggs should be able to start implementing the new changes within the next week."

"So the kid came up with a good plan, huh? And you're rewarding him with the job in Bart's department?" Sidney studied Adrien, then asked, "Don't answer that. Answer this. Who did you fuck last night and why didn't you tell me you were seeing someone new?"

After leaning back in his chair, Adrien stretched his arms over his head, and said, "I don't kiss and tell, Sidney."

"Since when?" Sidney looked surprised. "I've never known you not to brag about your conquests before. You've always let me live vicariously through your encounters."

"You know, if you'd stop working so hard, and enjoy your life, you wouldn't be alone," Adrien pointed out.

He chuckled when Sidney rolled his eyes. His friend had heard it all before. Adrien truly believed Sidney worked too hard. Adrien used to be like that, then he'd taken over at the company. His stress level had gone up, and he'd sworn to himself he wouldn't be like his father, who'd had a heart attack at fifty because he didn't know how to relax.

"Well, I'm not going to tell you anything about my bedroom activities." Adrien shrugged when Sidney protested. "It's not my place to say at the moment."

Sidney narrowed his eyes, and studied Adrien. "Is there something different about this guy? Or are you just embarrassed by him? Maybe he doesn't measure up to your mother's exacting standards as to who the Bellamy heir should date."

Someone clearing his throat brought their attention to the door where Patrick stood, and behind him, Adrien saw Ion with a stricken look on his face. Adrien jumped to his feet, but Ion disappeared before Adrien could go to him.

"Sir, your eleven o'clock appointment is here." Patrick didn't look happy either, and Adrien wondered if Ion had told his personal assistant what had happened between the two of them not just Friday night, but Saturday night as well.

"Oh, I haven't been able to talk to you since you sent Mr Vasile to interview with Bart and me. We're taking him on in a limited role until he's done with his MBA.

Once he has that, he'll take over Constance's position full time with all the benefits and salary." Sidney stood, then headed for the door. "Is that all right with you? I'll have Bart start showing him around."

"It's fine with me since that's why I sent him to you in the first place." Adrien rubbed the nape of his neck. "Patrick, can you show Miss Bronson to the conference room and see if she would like anything to drink?"

"Yes, sir." Patrick started to walk away, then Adrien stopped him.

"Wait. Can you see if Mr Vasile has time to meet with me some time this afternoon?"

Patrick glanced over, seemingly checking to make sure Sidney was out of earshot. "Are you sure that's a good idea, sir?"

"What do you mean?"

"Well, maybe you shouldn't spend too much time in each other's company while at work. I know what happened between the two of you over the weekend, and I don't want there to be a hint of Ion getting this promotion because he's sleeping with the boss." Patrick took a deep breath then stiffened like he was waiting for Adrien to yell at him.

"I want to talk to Ion about this situation, and trust me when I say I don't want to hurt Ion in any way." Adrien strolled over to where Patrick stood then leaned close to him. "I like him, Patrick. Probably more than I should for just having truly met him."

Patrick's eyes lit up, and Adrien had a feeling that he'd gained a supporter in his suddenly thought up plan to woo Ion.

"All right. I guess I'll have to trust you for now, but know this. You better not treat him like you're ashamed to be seen with him. He's just as good as you are, even without your money." Patrick glared.

"I know that, and I won't ever be embarrassed by Ion or his family. I'm more likely going to be by my own family." Adrien shook his head. "Now, just go and talk to Ion for me. I have to discuss some things with Miss Bronson."

Patrick nodded then left. Adrien inhaled sharply, having the sudden thought that maybe having a relationship with someone who worked for him wasn't the best idea in the world. Yet he couldn't get rid of the feeling that Ion was going to end up meaning more to him than any other man Adrien had ever dated. That scared him a little because Ion wasn't Adrien's usual type.

Adrien always dated men who were either in the same social circle as he was, or he dated younger men looking for sugar daddies. Too many times he'd found out his lover dated him because of his name and fortune. Adrien hadn't had to pay for sex since he'd started having it. Being good looking and rich made getting a person into bed really easy.

Yet something about Ion told Adrien his money didn't impress the younger man, and for the first time, Adrien might be judged by the kind of man he was, and not the amount in his bank account.

He grabbed the files he needed, then headed to meet with his eleven o'clock about the company her family wanted to purchase from Bellamy International.

* * * *

"Mr Bellamy, the newest troubleshooter is here to meet you."

Ion rolled his eyes at Patrick, not liking his best friend's smirk.

"Send him in, Patrick, and remember your job depends on you keeping secrets."

"Yes, sir." Patrick grinned at Ion. "You can go in now."

"Thanks," Ion said as he passed Patrick's desk.

Patrick reached out to catch his hand, stopping him. "Congratulations, Ion. Not only on the job. I knew you were right for each other. You just had to get a chance to see it."

Ion gave Patrick a quick hug. "I really do thank you, Patrick, and don't worry, you'll get your chance."

Patrick patted his back, then Ion entered Adrien's office. His lover stood in front of his desk, arms crossed as he waited for Ion to approach him.

"What are you thinking right now?" Ion asked, noticing the sudden gleam in Adrien's eye.

His lover leered. "I'm thinking how gorgeous you look in that suit, and how hot it would be to bend you over this desk and fuck you here in the office."

Ion's cock grew hard, and he swallowed his groan of need. God, what he would give to have that happen. He stepped closer to Adrien, resting his hand on Adrien's chest.

"While I'd love nothing more than to have you do that, we both know it won't be happening any time soon."

Adrien pouted. "Why not? As long as we lock the door, no one will know."

Ion gave Adrien an incredulous stare. "Seriously? The way you shout and grunt when we have sex? I doubt very much they'd be able to ignore that."

"Honey, I can be quiet given the right incentive," Adrien informed him.

Ion chuckled. "I'm sure you can, but not here and not now. While we both know you promoted me before we ever even kissed, there would be others in this company who'd accuse me of sleeping my way to this position."

"Is that why you want to keep our relationship a secret? Because you're afraid of what people might think?"

Ion couldn't tell how Adrien thought about that. There wasn't any inflection in his voice. After reaching up to touch Adrien's face, Ion trailed his fingers over Adrien's cheekbones.

"I am worried, but not for myself. I don't ever want you to get the reputation that you could be influenced by personal connections to make business decisions." Ion smiled. "You've never done it before."

"Do you ever plan on telling anyone?" Adrien asked.

Nodding, Ion pushed up on his toes to brush a kiss over Adrien's lips. "One day soon, I'll be shouting it from the rooftops. I'm not ashamed to be dating you, Adrien. Not one little bit. I'd just like to wait a while longer, and make sure we're going to last before making a public announcement."

He stared at Adrien, hoping he understood what he was trying to say. Finally Adrien sighed.

"All right, but even though we're keeping it a secret, you're not allowed to see other men."

Like that would happen. Adrien's command caused a tidal wave of happiness to rush over Ion. While he'd known Adrien cared for him, he'd been afraid Adrien would want to see other people to maintain their cover.

He wrapped Adrien in a tight embrace before whispering, "My body is reserved for you. It's a secret I'll find very difficult to keep."

Ion kissed Adrien, and as it deepened, he couldn't help smiling inside. Who would've thought find a solution to a plant closing and saving jobs would lead him to the possible love of his life?

When Adrien slid his hands around Ion's waist, Ion stepped back and shook his head. "We really can't be doing any of that in the office."

"No one will care," Adrien said.

"We've already discussed it. You might think they won't care, but I guarantee you, the ones who wanted my job will care, and they'll gossip about how I got the job." Ion took another step back, trying to remove the temptation of Adrien's body and lips. "I should get back to my new office."

Adrien didn't look happy. "I guess so. What time do you get home from class?"

"Ten." Ion reached the door, then turned to look at Adrien. "Why?"

"I thought I'd come over, and spend some time with you. Is that okay?"

Ion smiled at the hesitant tone in Adrien's question. He probably never felt nervous about anything in his life, yet he was worried Ion might say no about him stopping by later.

"If you come around ten-thirty, I should have my notes written up by then. We can make out on the couch." Ion winked, then left.

"You shouldn't tease the boss man," Patrick said.

"I think he needs to be teased, at least when we're alone together. I wouldn't dream of doing it here while we're at work. He's the boss, and deserves my respect." Ion grinned. "Oh, can we meet for dinner tomorrow? I have class tonight, then someone's coming over."

Patrick's eyebrows shot up, and his gaze shot over to where Adrien left his office. "Oh, right. Sure. We'll meet up for food tomorrow, and you're going to spill your guts about this whole thing."

Adrien nodded at them both, but showing no more interest in either of them than he would've any other day. Ion forced himself not to stare at Adrien's ass as he strolled down the hall toward Sidney's office.

"You need to get back to work," Patrick reminded him.

"Right. There's a lot of stuff backed up that I need to look at." Ion headed toward the elevators. "I'll talk to you later."

"You most certainly will."

* * * *

Later on, Ion stumbled out of the elevator to shuffle to his apartment door. He juggled his messenger bag, mail and the take-out Chinese he'd grabbed at the corner restaurant while trying to get his key out of his jacket pocket.

"How about I take something for you?"

He jumped and almost dropped everything when Adrien spoke from just behind him. Ion turned to see Adrien smile, then reach to take the Chinese from his hands.

"I would've brought food if I had known you'd be hungry," Adrien commented as Ion managed to get his door unlocked.

"I left work late, and didn't have time to pick up anything to eat before class. I thought I'd have time to eat it before you got here." After shoving the door open, he gestured for Adrien to go in. "It's not much, but it's mine and I can pay the rent on it without panicking every month about it."

"You should be able to find a bigger place in a better neighborhood now that you got a promotion and raise." Adrien strolled into the apartment like he owned it, and Ion rolled his eyes at the man's inherent arrogance.

"No, I won't." Ion let his bag drop on the floor next to the small table in the hallway. He set his keys and wallet in the misshapen bowl that sat in the middle of a white lace doily.

Adrien had gone into Ion's kitchen, then glanced back around the edge of the doorway. "Why not? I'm sure this place is nice and all, but wouldn't you want something bigger and more modern?"

After stripping off his jacket, Ion hung it up in the closet. He chuckled. "What would I do with more space? There's only me here. Sure the neighborhood isn't the best, but I'm all right with that. The extra money I get from my raise is going toward paying off my student loans and helping my parents with some of their bills."

Ion wandered in to see Adrien dishing out the food. The man seemed very at home in Ion's kitchen.

"Right." Adrien picked up the plates before turning to look at Ion. "You should grab the drinks. I brought a bottle of wine, which isn't supposed to be drunk with take-out Chinese, but I won't tell anyone if you won't."

Ion snatched up the bottle, glasses and the corkscrew, then followed Adrien out to his dining table. It wasn't that big, and Adrien had to shove some of Ion's books out of the way. After setting the plates down, Adrien took the wine from Ion, then opened it.

Ion sat, too hungry to argue with Adrien about his high-handedness. He took his first bite of General Tso' Chicken, and moaned. Adrien laughed as he pushed a glass of wine over to Ion.

"If you like this, just wait until I take you to China, and you can have authentic Chinese food. It's really not the same as what we get here." Adrien took a careful bite of his. He chewed, then after swallowing, he commented, "It's not bad."

"When you take me to China? Are there any business trips I should know about?" Ion took a sip and had to admit it was some of the best tasting he'd ever had. Of course, Adrien had probably spent hundreds of dollars on it while the most Ion ever spent on a bottle was twenty dollars, if he wanted the good stuff at the grocery store.

"Not yet anyway." Adrien looked at him with a slight smile. "I was talking out of hand, I guess. It's too soon to be planning joint trips, huh?"

"A little bit." Ion shook his head. "This is only our third date, even though we spent last weekend together. I don't usually rush into things, and don't jump into bed with guys I just met."

"Just met? We've known each other for over a year," Adrien pointed out before taking a sip of the wine.

Ion raised his eyebrows at Adrien's statement. "We barely talked for that entire year because you were my boss and I was a mail clerk. It wasn't like we were chatting at the water cooler before you asked me out."

Adrien frowned. "Chatting at the water cooler? Do people still do that? And I'm the boss. I couldn't really show you favor by singling you out for talks. No matter how much I wanted to."

"Really?" Ion picked up a piece of chicken with his chopsticks. He chewed while he thought about the year he'd worked in the mailroom, delivering letters and files to the different floors. He tried to pick out any signal Adrien might have sent him about being attracted to him, and he couldn't think of one.

"Yes. You're fucking gorgeous, Ion. What red-blooded male in his right mind wouldn't want to date you or just talk to you?" Adrien reached over to cover Ion's hand with his. "I'm glad we are spending time together like this. The sex is great, and I'm definitely looking forward to having more of it, but I want to get to know you as a person as well."

Ion turned his hand over then entwined his fingers with Adrien's. "I'm glad to know it's not just my body you want."

He took a deep breath, hoping that what he was about to ask wasn't going to backfire in his face. "I wondered if you'd like to go with me to my parents' house next Sunday."

"Really? Now you want me to meet your parents?" Adrien looked shocked.

Ion pulled away, letting it drop into his lap. "Is it too soon? I know I said we should wait until we'd been dating for a while longer, but I think it'll go just as well if we did it now, than if we waited."

After standing, Adrien walked around the table to crouch next to Ion. He took both of Ion's in his, and smiled at him. "No, it's not too soon. I'm just surprised because most guys either don't want me to meet their parents because they're embarrassed of where they came from, or they drag me around to show me off to everyone they know."

"To prove they have what it takes to land a rich handsome boyfriend?" Ion shook his head. "That's not why I want you to meet them."

Adrien kissed Ion quickly, then said, "I know."

"How would you know that? Like you said, we're just getting to know each other outside of work and bed. I could very well be taking you to my parents' to show you off." Ion frowned, not liking the idea that Adrien'd been used like that.

Adrien shrugged. "Just a gut feeling, I guess. You don't strike me as the kind of person who cares about things like wealth and power. Not saying that you don't like money, and wouldn't mind being well-off yourself, but it doesn't obsess you like some of the men I've met."

He wanted a happy medium between the two, because neither one sounded like it was a healthy way to live.

"Thanks for realizing that about me. I wouldn't want you to think I'm with you simply because of your money or your looks. Though you being walking eye candy does help," Ion teased before kissing Adrien back.

"Hmm..." Adrien hummed as they kissed, then he slid his arm around Ion's waist to pull him from the chair.

They tumbled into a heap on the floor, Ion on top of Adrien, but they continued to make out. Ion settled between his thighs, then rocked his hips into Adrien's groin. He groaned at the hard length that met his erection. His lover arched his back, pressing their lower halves together.

Grunting, Ion rubbed against Adrien, but when his elbow hit the table leg, he stopped. He rocked back on his heels, then stood. Ion held out his hand to help Adrien off the floor.

"I'm too old to be messing around on the floor. Maybe even the couch. I want my bed when you fuck me."

Adrien wrapped his arm around Ion's waist. "What if I want you to fuck me?"

Ion looked at him. "Are you serious?"

"Why wouldn't I be?" Adrien looked puzzled for a moment, then his expression cleared. "Unless you're a dedicated bottom?"

"No. I like to fuck and be fucked. Either way as long as we both get off, I'm happy." Ion nuzzled Adrien's jaw. "Let's go to bed."

"Wait. Do you have any homework that needs to be done? I don't want you to get in trouble for not having it done." Adrien gestured toward Ion's messenger bag.

"Don't worry. It's just reading, and I can do that at lunch tomorrow." Ion wasn't interested in stuff he could do without too much trouble the next day. He wanted Adrien in bed as soon as possible.

Ion encouraged Adrien to move toward the bedroom, and his soft mattress. "I have supplies in my room, Adrien."

"Then let's go."

Adrien's smile caused Ion's heart to skip a beat and his cock hardened even more at the sight. There was a hint of arrogance in the expression, yet there was also a glimpse of uncertainty in his eyes. Ion wasn't entirely sure what Adrien would be nervous about, but he planned on erasing it from Adrien's mind.

Ion escorted Adrien to his bedroom, not worried about whether it was neat or not. They were going to mess up the sheets anyway, so who cared if they were clean. He stumbled over a shoe on the floor by his bed, then landed on his mattress, tangled up in Adrien's arms.

Adrien wiggled and shifted until he was lying on top of Ion. He spread his thighs, letting Adrien wedge himself between them. They rocked together, and Ion groaned as their groins rubbed against each other. All he could think about at that moment was being naked, and feeling Adrien's body pressed to his.

"We need to be naked for the rest of this. I don't want to come in my pants." Ion tugged on Adrien's shirt.

"All right, but you shouldn't have pulled me down on top of you, or I would've been undressed by now." Adrien winked as he jumped to his feet.

Ion laughed. "Sorry I was so clumsy."

He stripped, tossing his clothes all over the room. Adrien was more meticulous about undressing, but of course, since his shirt probably cost more than all of the clothes in Ion's closet. God knew it would've cost Ion at least three months' rent to afford Adrien's suit.

Adrien placed his shoes under the chair in the corner, then folded his clothes before lying them on the seat. Ion was on the bed with the blankets and top sheet pulled to the foot of the mattress when Adrien finished. He stroked his cock, and Adrien studied him for a moment.

"Where are the supplies?"

"In a box under the bed." Ion gestured vaguely toward the floor.

"You couldn't have put them in a more convenient place like your nightstand or something like that?"

Ion watched as Adrien knelt by the bed to reach under, then pull out the box Ion kept his condoms and lube in.

"Your mom doesn't come over to your place very often, does she?" Ion stared at him as Adrien opened the top to grab a strip of condoms and the bottle.

Chapter Six

Adrien paused in the middle of tearing one of the packets off the strip to think about what Ion had said. *Your mother must not come and visit very often.* He shuddered at the thought of his mother going anywhere near his supplies. He tried to count how many times his parents had been to his apartment in the city. Maybe once when he first moved in there, but after that, they always stayed in their own place when they came to Manhattan, or he'd go out to their place in the Hamptons to visit.

He wasn't close to most of his family, though he got along best with his father, maybe because Adrien was more like his father than his mother. His siblings didn't work, relying on the money the corporation brought in to keep them in the life they've become accustomed to. Oh, they did charity work, or at least his sister did. His brother spent his time jet setting from one fun place to another.

Adrien and his father often discussed what they should do about Alain, but Mother always managed to distract his father before anything could be done.

Adrien had given up hope of his brother ever growing up. Then his father would get talking about his racing team, and Adrien would just let it all go.

His parents rarely met any of the men Adrien dated. Maybe it was because secretly he was embarrassed— either by his lovers or by his parents. He'd never been able to figure out which one it was.

Ion shifted on the bed, and Adrien found his gaze landing on Ion's cock. Why was he thinking about his family when he had something much more tempting spread out in front of him?

"How about we don't talk about our mothers in the bedroom, huh?" He climbed onto the bed, then straddled Ion's hips. After handing Ion the lube, he tore open the foil packet to get the rubber out. "Why don't you get me ready? I've been thinking about riding you since last weekend."

"You don't bottom very often, do you?" Ion grinned as he popped open the top of the slick. He squirted some on his fingers before closing it, then setting it aside.

Adrien shook his head. "Not really, but it's not because I don't want to get fucked. Most of the time, I guess, the men who go out with me expect me to top because of who I am and what I do."

Ion rubbed his fingers together, spreading the lube over them. "Being the CEO of a Fortune 100 company makes you a take-charge kind of guy, and most guys would think you wouldn't want to give up your control, even in the bedroom."

"That might be more true than I think, but I still do like to get fucked hard and fast sometimes." Adrien leered at Ion before turning around, presenting his ass to Ion while grasping his shaft with his hand. "Why don't you get me ready?"

"Yes, sir." Ion smacked his butt before running his fingers along Adrien's crease. "I always thought you had a great backside. Those Italian suits of yours certainly show it off nicely, and now being up close and personal with it, I've decided it's a shame you keep it covered."

Adrien shook his ass in Ion's face. "I can't very well walk around the office naked, Ion."

"True. No one would get any work done." Ion caressed Adrien's hole, and Adrien gasped.

It had been a long time since anyone besides himself had touched that most private of places. Adrien liked how it felt, but he wanted to get his mouth on Ion, so he flipped over. He arched his back, then focused his attention on Ion's cock.

He took Ion's length in, wanting to take his mind off any sort of commitment toward Ion just yet. Adrien knew it was coming because he already felt differently about Ion than any of his other lovers, but he wasn't ready to make the kind of serious commitment no protection would entail.

"Hmm…your mouth is almost as nice as your ass."

Adrien tensed slightly as Ion pressed one of his fingers into Adrien's. He appreciated the fact that Ion invaded him slowly and carefully, understanding that Adrien would be tight after not having bottomed for a long time.

Somehow they managed to get into a rhythm, him sucking on Ion's cock and Ion stretching Adrien's hole. He got lost in the feel of Ion's fingers relaxing him, and how Ion's erection filled his mouth. Pleasure simmered under his skin, building and expanding until he thought his flesh would split from the pressure.

He groaned as Ion removed his fingers from his inner passage, then patted his butt cheek.

"Turn around. I want you to come on my cock, and I'm pretty sure you're close to it."

Adrien shifted, allowing Ion to slide out of his mouth then slipped a condom on Ion. After swinging around, he grasped Ion's shaft, holding it in position while he slowly lowered himself down on it. Ion held his hips to help balance him as he settled. Adrien bit his lip, loving the way it felt having Ion stuff him full.

He paused once Ion's hard-on was inside him. Bracing his hands on Ion's chest, he stared down into Ion's dark brown eyes. Concern showed in them, as well as lust and an emotion that looked very much like love.

"Are you okay?" Ion stroked Adrien's hips, seeming to try and soothe the small twist of pain from him.

Adrien bit his lip, thinking about it for a moment before he nodded. "I'm all right. Feeling really good, actually."

He tightened his muscles around Ion's shaft. Ion gasped, and Adrien grinned. He pushed up until just the tip of Ion's cock was inside him, then he dropped back down, almost slamming their bodies together.

"You might want to take it a little slower, since you haven't done this in a while," Ion suggested.

Adrien shook his head. "I'm fine, Ion."

He began to move up and down, enjoying the sensation of Ion sliding in and out of his ass. Adrien jerked a little when Ion wrapped one of his hands around Adrien's shaft, letting it fuck his fist.

Losing himself in the pleasure of the moment, he wallowed in the way Ion made him feel. He could see why so many guys enjoyed getting fucked. The fullness in his passage, and how Ion drove his need higher each time he nailed Adrien's gland.

His cock swelled even more as his balls drew tight to his body. His passion built at the base of his spine, then exploded through him. Cum spilled out to cover Ion's hand and his stomach.

Adrien groaned and trembled as his climax rocketed through him. His muscles massaged Ion's length, drawing a low moan from him as well. Ion let go of Adrien, then gripped his hips to start driving up into him. Bracing his hands on Ion's chest, he rode out his climax along with Ion's.

When all the strength drained from his body, Adrien collapsed on top of Ion, who grunted, but didn't push him away. Adrien sighed as Ion encircled his waist to pull him close. He did wrinkle his nose at the stickiness between them, trying to make a note to clean up before they fell asleep. As much as he liked Ion, he didn't want to be stuck to him in the morning.

* * * *

His alarm buzzed, and Adrien reached to turn it off. Instead of hitting plastic, he hit warm flesh.

"Ow! What the hell?"

Opening his eyes, Adrien found himself looking into Ion's irritated eyes. Ion rubbed his shoulder where he'd smacked him. The alarm kept going off, and Adrien groaned.

"Can you shut that off?"

"Sorry."

The mattress shifted when Ion moved, and once the noise went silent, Adrien sat up in the bed. He stretched his arms over his head. Ion rolled out from under the covers, then stood. Adrien watched as Ion scratched himself before heading to the bathroom.

After standing, Adrien started to dress, pulling on his clothes while he listened to Ion finish up in the bathroom. He'd just completed his call to his driver when Ion came out. The man stopped when he spotted Adrien standing there dressed except for his shoes.

"You leaving already?"

He tried to ignore how Ion looked, naked and his cock half-hard. They needed to get to work and he didn't want Ion in trouble for being late. It didn't matter what time Adrien got in. Being the boss had its privileges.

"You have to go, and I'm going home and change before I go into the office." Adrien leaned over to brush a kiss over Ion's lips. "If I take a shower with you, I'm not going to be interested in anything except taking you back to bed."

Ion nodded. "You're right about that. You should probably head out. I'll see you at work."

"Wait. Before I head out, I want to know what made you change your mind about me meeting your parents. You said you thought we should be together for a month or so before I went to Sunday dinner with you." Adrien took Ion's hand, then squeezed it gently.

"I had a talk with my brother about you. Not you specifically. He doesn't know who you are, but he knows I'm seeing someone. Anyway, I said something about bringing you to meet them, and he told me not to push it." Ion frowned.

"Not push what?" Adrien shook his head.

Ion glanced away, then met his gaze again. "My parents know I'm gay. I told them when I left for college. I admitted it to myself when I was like fifteen, just never said anything to them before because I knew they'd have problems with it. They're old-fashioned, and still believe that I just need to meet the right girl to prove that I'm not gay."

Adrien blinked as he worked through what Ion said. He had issues with his parents, but they'd never once told him he just needed a wife and everything would be fine. Whether they were happy about him being gay or not, they never said a word to him about it. Of course, he didn't care how they felt either, and hadn't since he went to boarding school.

But Ion obviously did care about his parents and their opinions, though it sounded like Ion was reaching his own line in the sand.

"I want them to meet you, Adrien, and I've made the decision that if they can't accept you as family because I care for you, then I don't want to be a part of their family anymore." Ion shoved his free hand through his hair. "Why is it okay for them to accept Bogdan's wife, but not you simply because you're a man, and it wasn't done in their time?"

Adrien slid his hand around to cup the back of Ion's head before bringing it forward to rest their foreheads together. "Don't get upset about it, honey. They're your parents, and they love you. Maybe it's not unconditional like we're taught to expect from our family, but they still care about you."

Ion shrugged. "Maybe they do, but they don't really show it. All I hear is why am I working as a mailman when I could be making more money doing anything else. They don't seem to understand that I'm doing what I want to get more experience. Sure, it might not be as important as being a doctor or lawyer, but it's a step on the path to a better job for me."

He got Ion's thinking on the whole working from the bottom up in a business. His father had groomed him to take his place from the moment he came out of his mother's womb.

"Have you ever brought someone home to meet them?" Adrien stepped away when his phone buzzed. He checked the screen to find a text from his driver that he was downstairs waiting. "Can we have the rest of this conversation today at lunch?"

"Are you sure we should be having lunch together if we're trying to keep things quiet at the company?" Ion frowned.

Adrien grimaced as he headed toward the door. "You're right. What time do you get home from school tonight?"

"By ten. Are you going to be here?" Ion followed him, then put a hand on his arm to stop him.

"If you want me to be. I don't want to distract you from homework or anything. I know getting your Masters is important to you. I also don't want to give you any reason to stop seeing me." Adrien covered Ion's hand with his.

Ion pursed his lips as he seemed to be thinking about it. "How about I call you when I get home? I'm going to have some stuff to read and a paper to write. I won't want to do it if you're here."

"I can do that." He kissed Ion again, then forced himself to leave.

* * * *

At nine o'clock that night, Adrien's phone rang, and he answered without checking the ID on the screen.

"Hello?"

"Adrien dear, this is your mother." His mother always said that when she called, like he wouldn't recognize her voice or something.

"Yes, Mother. I have heard your voice before," he commented as he flopped back on his couch. He'd been hoping that Ion would call early, but he guessed his lover wasn't home from school yet.

"No need to be sarcastic, Adrien." She sighed like he was the most annoying thing she had to deal with that day.

Glad that she couldn't see him, he rolled his eyes. "Sorry, Mother. How was your day?"

She always liked it when he asked her that. Of course, he didn't care about anything she did, but Mother liked to tell him about her charity work and social events.

"It was very nice. I had a board meeting for the Children's Hospital Fundraiser. You will be there of course. I told them you'd buy two tickets." Before he could say yes or no, she continued, "Also, your sister and her husband will be in town Friday night. I will expect you to be here at six for cocktails."

"Of course, I'll buy tickets to the fundraiser." And though he wanted to say no, he went on to say, "I'll be happy to join you and the others for dinner. I'll be bringing a friend."

He swore he could hear her ears perk up when he said 'friend'.

"A friend? Really? You haven't brought one of your boys home to meet us. This must be serious. I'll inform your father."

The way she said 'boy' put his teeth on edge. "He's not a boy, Mother. Ion is finishing up his Masters in Business and already has a full-time job waiting for him when he does. I would like you to treat him with respect."

"Of course, we'll respect the young man. I simply say boy because I know the type of man you've dated before, and I'm sure you knew none of them were really our kind of person." Mother sighed. "I assume he's more our type because you're actually bringing him to have us meet him. Should I have your brother come to dinner as well?"

"No!" Adrien didn't want Alain there. His brother wasn't a shining example of the family. Well, to be honest, none of his siblings were really people he was proud of.

He liked Amelia for the most part, and her husband wasn't too bad. Adrien thought about the fact that he should make more of an effort to spend time with his family. They weren't the most loving group, but maybe all they needed was someone to show them how.

"All right. I won't ask him. Goodness knows I have no idea where he is right now. That boy never calls. You'd think he was an orphan or something, the way he ignores his family."

He blocked out his mother's complaints about his brother. He could tell her where Alain was since he'd received a statement from a hotel in Monaco where his brother had run up a hefty bill from gambling and partying. Adrien had paid it, though he had wanted to refuse, but he didn't want to listen to both his mother and Alain complain about his being mean or jealous of his younger brother.

"So we'll see you at six, right?"

"Yes, Mother. Ion and I will be there at six." He silently asked Ion's forgiveness for including him without asking first.

"Why don't you plan on staying the weekend? Amelia and Jonathon will be here as well. It'll be nice to have most of my children home for my birthday." Mother laughed, and Adrien felt like a heel for not remembering that his mother's birthday was on Saturday.

"Are you having a party as usual?"

If she was, that meant he'd have to make sure Ion had a tuxedo to wear. His mother's parties were legendary in the Hamptons, and he didn't want Ion to feel any more out of place then he already would.

"Of course, dear. Why wouldn't I? Now you make sure to let Ion know he must dress appropriately. I'll see you Friday night, darling." She hung up.

After Adrien did the same, he threw his phone onto the cushions next to him. He groaned. *How am I going to tell Ion that the first time he meets my parents, it's for my mother's birthday? He's going to be livid.*

He snatched up his phone, then sent an email to himself to remember to pick up a bottle of his mother's favorite perfume and a box of the Swiss chocolate she loved. It was the same thing he always got her, but she seemed to enjoy the fact that he remembered she liked them.

Setting the phone back down, he shook his head. He was going to have to find Alain and make sure his brother got home in time for Mother's party. She might act like she didn't mind if he wasn't there, but Adrien knew it would hurt her feelings when her favorite child didn't make an appearance.

As Adrien thought up bribes he could offer Alain to get him home, his phone rang again. This time he checked the screen and saw Ion's name pop up. Smiling, he swiped his finger across the face.

"Hey there, honey. How was school?" He slowly slid until he rested on his back, staring up at the ceiling.

"Good. Had a pop quiz for some strange reason, but I did well on it. At least I knew all the material." Ion sounded tired. "How was your day?"

"Bought and sold a couple of companies. All in all, another profitable twenty-four hours." Adrien bit his lip, trying to figure out a way to bring up going to his parents' for the weekend.

Ion chuckled. "Not many people can say that without sounding obnoxiously pretentious."

He winced. "Did I? Probably sounded pretty arrogant, huh?"

"A little, but that's okay. I know you didn't mean it that way." Ion groaned like he was stretching or something. "I called my mama and told her that I'd be bringing you with me to dinner on Sunday."

"How did she react?"

"She got very quiet, then said she hoped you liked meatloaf." Ion sighed. "I hope you do too, because she can make a mean one. I swear Patrick is psychic when it comes to that. I guarantee he'll be standing at my door when I get home after dinner on Sunday. Mama always makes sure to send me home with my own container, just so Patrick will be able to have some."

Adrien couldn't remember the last time he had meatloaf. Probably not since he was a kid and eating dinner with the cook and his nanny in the kitchen. *Did I like it back then?* It hadn't made a lasting impression on him one way or the other, so he was willing to give it a try.

"I'm sure I'll love it, Ion. I'm not a picky eater, and anyway, I'll be there to meet your parents, not critique her cooking skills."

"I know that, but to my mama, food is important and if you don't like her cooking, she just might not like you." Ion exhaled loudly. "Hell, she might not like you even if you do like her meatloaf. All because you're a guy and she wants me to bring home a nice young lady she can teach how to make all my favorites."

Adrien smiled, then said, "If it'll make her happy, I'll take lessons from her every night of the week. I know this is going to be difficult for you, Ion, and I don't want to do anything that will upset either of your parents. How is your father going to take me showing up with you?"

"He has never really said anything to me about being gay. It's like as long as he doesn't discuss it, I'm straight. The weird thing is he's fine with Patrick. They talk about baseball, and he doesn't flinch if Patrick says something about how good players' asses look in those uniforms." Ion fell silent for a moment before continuing, "Of course, Patrick isn't his son, so it's different. He didn't have a hand in raising him and there's no feeling of failure."

He wanted to ask why Ion's father would think he failed with Ion somehow, but he wasn't ready to have that discussion. Not when his mind was on his own. "Speaking of parents, how would you like to come out to the Hamptons with me on Friday? We can go out and spend the weekend. Actually, having to come back for dinner with your family on Sunday would give us the perfect excuse to leave early."

"You want me to meet yours?" Ion sounded surprised.

"Yes. I told you I did. I know it's rather sudden, but my mother called to tell me she expected me for dinner on Friday. My sister, Amelia and her husband are going to be there. Also, I totally forgot that Saturday is my mother's birthday, and she usually throws a big party to celebrate. I'll be expected to stay for that as well."

Ion coughed, and Adrien wondered if his lover wasn't starting to panic a little.

"Don't worry. I'll buy you a tuxedo, so you won't have to fork out money for that."

"I can rent one. You don't have to pay for my clothes," Ion protested.

Adrien shook his head, even though Ion couldn't see him. "Oh no. We need to buy you one because my mother can spot a rented tux a mile away, and so can all her old biddie friends. They'll never let you live it down, and besides, if you and I continue dating, you'll be going to a lot of black tie functions with me. It's best to get a tux tailored for you now."

"Umm…"

"Please, Ion. If you want, you can pay me back for it. I'll even charge you interest, but I guarantee you'll feel better wearing a tux you own than a rented one. The people you're going to meet on Saturday can be some of the snobbiest people in the world. Trust me, I know. I grew up with a majority of them. I'm not helping my case at all, am I? Maybe I should just shut up now."

A soft laugh drifted over the phone, and he relaxed slightly. If Ion could laugh, then he wasn't too upset by Adrien's babbling.

"All right. I'll go with you, and I'll let you get my tux. But nothing else. I can pay for my own clothes. I'm not dating you so you can be my sugar daddy," Ion informed him.

"Thank you, Ion. I do appreciate you coming, and I promise we will leave as soon as we possibly can on Sunday." He really was happy that his lover had decided to come with him. Adrien did want Ion to meet his parents, even if he would prefer to do it a different way. He had a thought in his head that he'd invite his parents to the city for dinner, and they would meet at a restaurant where they had to be polite in public. That way his mother couldn't get too obnoxious.

Unfortunately, now they would be meeting them on their own territory, and his mother would have no restraints. He took a deep breath, not wanting to give even a hint that he wasn't in total control of every minute of his life.

"Well, you'll have to deal with my parents on Sunday night, so that'll go a little ways to making up for what I'm going to encounter this weekend," Ion teased.

"To be honest, I'm probably exaggerating a little about everything. It's just you're the first guy I've brought home to meet them, and I really want it to work out, so I'm panicking."

Ion grunted. "Huh. Who knew Adrien Bellamy, CEO extraordinaire, could get nervous about anything? Don't worry, dear. I won't hold your family against you as long as you don't hold mine against me."

"Deal." He heard Ion stifle a yawn. "Why don't you do whatever homework you have, then go to bed? We should go tomorrow night to give Salvatore as much time as possible to get it done before we leave on Friday."

"Good idea. I don't have class tomorrow night, so that'll be fine. Good night, Adrien. I'll see you tomorrow."

"Sweet dreams." He hung up, then headed to bed himself.

Chapter Seven

Ion glanced at Adrien as they entered the high-end clothing store. "What are we doing here? I thought we were going to dinner."

"We are, but remember we need to get some things for you." Adrien nodded toward the back of the store where an older man stood, obviously waiting for them.

"Some things? I thought we were just getting a tux for me." Ion looked around, then picked up a shirt. There wasn't a price tag on it, and Ion realized that he might not want to know how much the items in that store were.

"Remember you agreed to go to my parents this weekend, and attend my mother's birthday party. I'm afraid you're going to need another suit besides the tux. We dress for dinner." Adrien gripped Ion's elbow, escorting him up to the man. "Salvatore, I've brought you a new customer."

"You always do bring me the best looking men, Mr Bellamy." Salvatore grinned at Ion. "Come. You must undress, so I can get your measurements."

He dug in his heels, not letting either of them force him into doing something he wasn't sure of.

"We need to talk."

Adrien sighed, but nodded. "Can you give us a few minutes alone?"

"Certainly, sir." Salvatore stepped to the other side of the store to give them the illusion of privacy.

Ion pointed at the suit on the mannequin. "I'm not going to let you buy me a whole new wardrobe, Adrien. Not when I have a perfectly good suit at home. It might not be Armani or Calvin Klein, but it's nice and cost me one month's pay to buy it. It fits me just fine without having to be tailored."

Adrien took Ion's hands in his. "I know that, but I thought you might like a few things to help fit in better with my family. My mother is very judgmental. I don't want you to feel like you don't measure up to them."

"Just because my clothes aren't as nice as yours or theirs?" Ion shook his head. "It takes more than that to make a person, Adrien. I know who I am, and I don't need designer ones to make me equal to your parents. I agreed to a tuxedo. That's it."

He wasn't going to budge on it, no matter what Adrien said. If he started giving in, then pretty soon he'd have a better apartment, a whole new wardrobe, and no self-esteem. He would become like all those other beautiful men Adrien had brought to Salvatore to dress.

Adrien studied him, then nodded. "All right. I'll buy you the tuxedo, but you need a shirt, tie, cuff links, and shoes to go with them. Are you okay with me paying for those as well?"

"Not really, but I know when to stop protesting. You buy what you think I need for the party, but that's it.

The other stuff I have for the rest of the weekend will be fine, and if your mother doesn't like it, that's okay. I'm not falling in love with her. I'm falling in love with you, and you don't mind my clothes, do you?"

Blinking, Adrien shook his head. "I don't care what you wear. Hell, I'd rather you weren't wearing anything."

He blushed, but continued, "Then aside from the tux, the rest doesn't matter. I don't think you need to change how you dress to meet my parents. Though for God's sake, don't wear a suit. Jeans and a nice shirt will be fine. We don't dress for dinner at my house."

"Got it. We'll stop by my place on the way to your parents', and I'll change." Adrien waved Salvatore back over. "Now let Salvatore take your measurements, and we'll get you set up."

"Fine, but we're also going to have a conversation about all the other beautiful men you've brought here. Later." He eyed Adrien, who ducked his head a little.

"Yes, sir."

He endured getting measured, then pinned into a tux. Standing there like a sewing model, he listened to Salvatore and Adrien discuss fabric, cut and color. He really didn't understand why all of it was important, but Adrien believed it was, so he would deal with it.

When they finished and arranged to pick up their order on their way out of town on Friday, they headed to a nearby Thai restaurant. After they'd ordered, Ion looked at Adrien for a moment before he said, "How many of your lovers have you taken there?"

Adrien shrugged. "A few of them."

"What made you think I'd want to go somewhere you've taken other men whose wardrobes you've bought?"

"I didn't think about it. Salvatore is the best tailor in the city. He does all my suits, and I want you to have the best, so why wouldn't I take you there?" Adrien held up his hand, and Ion bit back what he was about to say. "I don't think you're like any of those other men. It's obvious you're not interested in me for my money or for whatever help I can give you in your career. I've kept our relationship quiet from the others at the office except for Patrick, and you're not bragging at the water cooler."

Ion shook his head. "I wouldn't brag anyway. Sharing my private life at work isn't something I do. The only reason Patrick would know anything is because we're best friends. If we weren't, he wouldn't know I was gay, much less dating anyone."

"I get it. The only reason anyone knows who I'm dating is because when I go out to social events, I get written up in the papers." Adrien looked like he had swallowed something unpleasant. "I hate to say this, but Sidney will be at my mother's party, and probably some of the other head officers at Bellamy."

Wincing, Ion fidgeted with his glass while he thought about all of his bosses knowing he was dating the top guy. "I guess we'll see how they react then. I'm not going to stop seeing you. If you start getting hassled about it, then I'll quit and get a job somewhere else. It's not like there aren't other jobs out there. I just chose your company because it has one of the best reputations in the business."

"I don't want you to have to quit. We'll see what we can do." Adrien reached out to pat his hand. "Let's not borrow trouble until we have to."

Ion wasn't interested in arguing anymore. They would deal with everything as it came. No point making himself crazy worrying about it.

"You're right."

They chatted about various things while they ate, then headed to Ion's place. Adrien had packed an overnight bag, so he wouldn't have to leave earlier than necessary. They would figure out how to explain showing up at the office at the same time in the morning. He wasn't going to pass up a chance to spend the night in his lover's arms just because he didn't want anyone to get suspicious.

Ion shut the door behind them, and Adrien shoved him back against the wood. He slid his hands into Adrien's hair, holding him still as he devoured Adrien's mouth. Ion wrapped his leg around Adrien's to bring their groins together.

"Fuck!" Ion let his head drop back to bounce against it. He arched his hips, loving the feel of their erections rubbing on each other.

Then the pressure was gone, and he looked down to see Adrien on his knees in front of him. He sucked in his stomach to allow Adrien room to undo his belt, then his button and zipper. Cool air washed over his cock as Adrien pushed his pants down to his knees. He smiled when his lover swallowed his entire length down.

"God, I love your mouth," Ion muttered while he began to slide in and out of Adrien, trying not to speed up. He didn't want to choke him.

Adrien cupped Ion's balls in one hand while sliding the other one around his hip to rub over his hole. Ion shuddered at the multiple sensations fighting to overwhelm him. Then when Adrien pressed his finger into Ion, his pleasure grew. Need sprang from every spot where Adrien touched him, then pooled along his nerve endings.

Ion thrust forward before pushing back, fucking Adrien's mouth while impaling himself on his lover's fingers. His entire body tensed as his climax raced through him, and he flooded Adrien's throat with his cum. Adrien swallowed as much as he could, but a little bit trailed from the corners of his lips.

Once his orgasm ended, Ion's knees went weak, allowing him to sink to the floor. He watched Adrien rip open his own pants, then start pumping his cock. Ion summoned the energy to wrap his hand around Adrien's shaft before joining in on the jerking off.

Adrien's head dropped back and he moaned loudly as he came, spilling his seed all over their hands and his pants. He kept the motion up until he was sure Adrien was done. Then he collapsed against the wall, and Adrien curled up in his arms.

"We should probably clean up, and toss your pants in the washer," he murmured.

Adrien caressed Ion's thigh. "I think these are a lost cause. I'll just throw them away. It's not like I don't have more at home."

Ion rolled his eyes at the idea of wasting a perfectly good pair of slacks just because Adrien didn't want to take the time to wash them. "I think we can rinse them in the sink and get the worst out. Then you can drop them off at the dry cleaners tomorrow."

"Fine. Whatever. Do we have to do it right now?" Adrien didn't seem inclined to move.

Laughing, Ion pinched Adrien's ass. "Yes, because I'm not taking a nap on the floor in front of my door. What if my mom shows up unannounced? There are some things a mother doesn't want to see her adult son doing."

"And sleeping half-clothed on the floor with his boyfriend is one of them," Adrien continued.

"Right." Ion took a deep breath, then pushed himself to his feet. He held out his hand for Adrien to take.

Once they were both up, Ion got their clothes mostly in order, then got them moving to the bathroom. He waited until they were both getting ready for bed before he grabbed Adrien's pants to wash them in the sink. Then he glanced at the tag on the waistband and shook his head.

"You're right. I think the best thing to do is just throw these out. I don't think there's any way to get cum out of silk, even if I do rinse it off," he called to Adrien.

"I told you." Adrien wandered back to lean against the doorframe, arms folded over his bare chest. "I know you think I'm just throwing money out, but like I said, I really do have plenty more in my closet at home. It's not like I'm going to throw these out, then run to Salvatore's to buy a new pair right away."

Ion frowned. "I just can't imagine not having to think about it before throwing something away. I didn't grow up with that kind of money."

He wadded the pants up in a ball before leaving the bathroom to walk to the kitchen area. After tossing them in the trash, he turned the lights out then joined Adrien in bed. He embraced his lover, entangling their arms and legs while laying his head on Adrien's shoulder.

"I'm not going to apologize for growing up with money, Ion. It's not something I could control." Adrien's voice rumbled against Ion's ear.

"I know, and I'm sorry. I'm going to work harder at not judging you because you aren't judging me," Ion promised, then he laughed. "It's not like I won't be making more money soon."

Adrien chuckled along with him. "You're right. Once you graduate, and start moving up the corporate ladder, you'll be making as much money as me."

He snorted. "I doubt that'll ever happen, but I'll be happy making enough to put some away for retirement and having a little left over for fun."

"Makes sense to me. Let's do our best to make that dream come true."

Ion listened as Adrien's breathing slowed and deepened until he was asleep. Staring up at the ceiling, Ion tried to imagine what Adrien's parents were like, but he drew a blank. He had never been on the executive floor when either Mr or Mrs Bellamy showed up.

Shit! He was going to have to talk to Patrick about what to get Mrs Bellamy for her birthday. He couldn't show up empty handed, though he was pretty sure Adrien would tell him he didn't have to get her anything.

Ion's mother would be very embarrassed if he were to show up to the Bellamy home without some kind of hostess gift. They might not have had much money, but his mother always managed to find something to take when they were guests in other people's houses.

Sighing, he shut his eyes. He needed to get some sleep or else he was going to be worthless at work and school tomorrow.

* * * *

Ion strolled out of Salvatore's shop with a garment bag over one shoulder and holding another one. Adrien's driver took them both from him to put into the trunk. He climbed into the backseat where Adrien was still on the phone with Winston Grollon, the head of the London office. Something had come up while they were on their way out of the city, and Adrien had to take the call.

After settling onto the seat beside Adrien, Ion rested his hand on his thigh, then turned to watch the buildings pass by as their driver took them out of New York on the way to the Hamptons. It was the first time he'd be visiting there, and he couldn't imagine what it would be like.

"I know it's important, Winston, but there's nothing I can do about it until Monday. Everything is closed for the weekend here. In fact, why aren't you in the country?" Adrien shot Ion a glance. "Oh, you are. Well, now that you've brought this to my attention, you can go have fun for the next three days. As soon as I get into the office on Monday, I'll take a look at the numbers and get back to you as soon as I can."

Winston must have gone on a tirade while Adrien's eyes widened and Ion could almost make out what the man was saying on the other end of the call. He frowned — from all of what Patrick had said about the man in charge of the European branch of Bellamy International, Winston Grollon was rather an even keel kind of guy, and wasn't prone to dramatics.

Adrien held the phone away from his ear for a second and stared at it. After he replaced, he cleared his throat before saying, "Win, stop and take a deep breath. I know that it isn't your fault, and I won't blame you, no matter what I find. You brought it to my attention as soon as you caught it. We're good. Now try and relax. All of this stress isn't good for you."

Shortly after that, Adrien hung up. He stuck his phone in his pocket while shaking his head. "Poor

Winston is freaking out. I've never heard him as upset as he was just then."

"What's going on?" Ion asked, then said, "Wait. Can you tell me about it or not?"

Adrien shrugged. "I don't see why I can't tell you. He found some discrepancies in the finances of one of the new companies we just purchased."

Ion nodded, but didn't ask any more.

"So did Salvatore have you try the tux on before you left with it?" Adrien seemed determined to not think about it.

"Of course he did. Everything fits just fine, and I have everything I need." He glanced down at his jeans. "Will we have enough time to change before dinner tonight?"

"Yes." Adrien covered his hand with his and squeezed. "I made sure we left early enough to give us time. We won't be able to take showers or anything, but change…yes."

"Good. These are my best jeans, but I got the feeling your parents wouldn't be thrilled to have me show up in them." He winked at Adrien.

Adrien smiled. "I can't wait to show you around the compound. Spent a lot of weekends out there, sailing as often as I could."

He slid his hand up Adrien's thigh. "What relaxes you now?"

"Doing you." Adrien grabbed him then pushed him down on the seat.

They proceeded to make sure Adrien was very relaxed by the time they arrived to the Bellamy compound four hours later. Traffic had been a bit heavy as they were leaving the city.

When the driver pulled the car to a stop in front of the biggest house Ion had ever seen, Ion finished buttoning his jeans back up. He made sure he was put together before he stepped from the vehicle. Adrien followed him, then they stood staring up at the house.

"Holy fucking Christ! This is your get-away home?" Ion thought his eyes might pop out of his head as he tried to take in the giant mansion.

"It's not mine, and actually my parents live here full time now," Adrien informed him as he took Ion's elbow in his hand. "Let's go in. Dylan, can you make sure our bags get to our suite?"

"Certainly, sir. Then I'm taking off until you call me on Sunday," Dylan said before turning away.

"You gave your driver the weekend off?" Ion knew it really wasn't important in the grand scheme of things, but he was still trying process the enormity of the building before him.

Adrien shrugged one shoulder. "Sure. Why wouldn't I? It's not like we'll need him. If we go anywhere tomorrow, I can drive."

Ion nodded, then his gaze went to the front door where a man stood, having just opened the door. "That doesn't look like your father."

"No. That's Mason, my parents' butler." Adrien took the front steps quickly before coming to a stop in front of the older man. "Mason, it's good to see you."

"Nice to see you as well, sir. I'm glad you could make it out this weekend." Mason bowed slightly.

Adrien gestured for Ion to join him. "Do you really think I would miss my mother's party?"

Mason snorted, then glanced over his shoulder as if checking to make sure no one was behind him. "If you could, I'm sure you would, sir."

"You know me too well."

Ion was surprised when Adrien hugged the guy before grabbing Ion's hand to drag him in front of Mason.

"This is my boyfriend, Ion Vasile. Ion, this is Mason. He's been the butler here for as long as I can remember."

That would explain why he seemed so friendly with the man. Adrien had probably spent more time with Mason than with his own father. Ion held out his hand.

"It's nice to meet you, sir."

"Please, just call me Mason. And likewise, sir. I'm glad Adrien is finally bringing someone home for us to meet." Mason stepped back and motioned for them to come in. "Your parents are getting ready. You have enough time to change before cocktails."

"Thanks, Mason."

Ion let Adrien lead the way upstairs to the left wing of the house. Dylan nodded to them as they passed in the hallway. Adrien opened the double doors at the end of the corridor.

"This is my suite when I stay here. Dylan should've put our bags in the bedroom over there." Adrien pointed to the door on the left. "The bathroom is on this side." He gestured toward the door closest to them on the right. "I'm going to wash up, then change."

He followed Adrien in, not surprised when he spotted two sinks and the large shower. "No expense was spared in building this place, was there?"

"Why would there be? It's not like my father didn't have the money, and my mother has very expensive taste."

They cleaned up, then dashed across the sitting room area to the bedroom where their bags had been set on the king sized bed. Dylan had taken the time to hang up Ion's garment bag, so Ion went to get his suit out, plus grab the hostess gift Patrick had helped him pick out.

He dressed quickly, then checked his reflection in the mirror. "Is this okay?"

Adrien trailed his gaze from the top of Ion's head to the tips of his shoes. Ion relaxed when he smiled and walked over to kiss his cheek.

"You look perfect, and Mother is going to love you." Adrien gave him a wink. "If she doesn't, who cares? Because I do and I'm the only one that matters."

Ion grabbed Adrien by the head, and brought their lips together in a crushing kiss. He needed the sting to remind him of that fact. They took the stairs together, then Adrien went right before heading toward the back of the building. Mason stood next to a pair of French doors done in beautiful stain glass.

"Cocktails are being served out on the veranda, sir." Mason opened one of the doors for them.

"Thank you, Mason." Adrien went through and Ion nodded at Mason before walking outside.

Taking a deep breath of the bracing salt-tinged sea air, Ion gripped the bottle of wine in his hand while approaching the rather distinguished looking couple Adrien greeted.

"Mother." Adrien kissed the air close to his mother cheek before turning to shake his father's hand. "Father."

"Adrien dear, so wonderful of you to come join us this weekend." She smiled at Ion, and said, "You must be Ion Vasile, my son's companion."

"He's my boyfriend, Mother. Calling him my companion makes it sound like both of us are in our nineties on our way to the home." Adrien held out his hand for Ion. "Ion, this is my father, Robert, and my mother, Alyssa."

"Sir." Ion shook Robert's hand, then turned to hold out the bottle of wine to Alyssa. "I understand this is your favorite wine, ma'am."

Alyssa took his gift, and read the label. Her blue eyes weren't nearly as brilliant as her son's, but Ion could see where he got them from. Her unlined face lit up with joy before she leaned forward to kiss his cheek.

"Thank you so much, Ion. You're right. This is one of my favorites." She handed it off to Mason. "We'll have some of that right now."

"Yes, ma'am."

She slid her hand through Ion's arm, drawing him close to her as they moved toward a cluster of chairs at the edge of the veranda. "Now where did you and Adrien meet? He's told us nothing about you."

Ion glanced back, but Adrien was talking to his father. Alyssa laughed as she motioned for Ion to sit.

"They'll be talking business for a little while. Robert always has to check in on the company when Adrien comes for a visit." She patted his hand. "It's nice to have someone else to chat with while they're doing this."

Ion wished they'd thought to discuss their story of meeting. He wasn't sure if Adrien wanted his parents to know how they met. "We met at the company. I used to work in the mail room, but I got a promotion."

"The mail room? Really?" Her perfectly arched eyebrows rose a little. "What kind of promotion?"

"I just started working as a troubleshooter. Part time until I get my degree from Columbia Business School." He bit his lip, not wanting to babble, simply because he was scared that she would discover he wasn't good enough for her son.

"Columbia? That's a nice school. Thank you, Mason." Alyssa took a glass from the tray Mason held. "I'm not sure what a troubleshooter is. My interests lie in different directions than my husband and son."

"Adrien said you are involved in a lot of charity work," Ion brought up. Of course, it wasn't Adrien who'd told him that. He'd gleaned all the information he could about Adrien's parents from Patrick.

A genuine smile lit up Alyssa's face as she began telling Ion about all of her charities. He found the variety of them interesting, and was amazed how she managed to keep them all separate in her mind.

Adrien and Robert joined them as Alyssa wound down, and Ion smiled at Adrien when his lover touched his shoulder before sitting next to him. Alyssa tapped Robert's hand to draw his attention.

"Ion works at Bellamy with Adrien. He's a new troubleshooter."

Robert frowned. "Dating inside the company, Adrien? Not something I'd advise."

"It works for us, Father. Have Amelia and Jonathon arrived yet?"

Alyssa went with Adrien's change of subject. "They just got here a few minutes ago. They were going to change, then join us." She took a sip of the wine before smiling at Ion. "This is marvelous, Ion."

"Thank you, ma'am. I'm glad it was the right kind." He would take all the credit for the wine if it helped her like him and maybe get Adrien to relax.

"Do you know anything about car racing, Ion?" Robert asked.

Ion pursed his lips then admitted, "Not one thing, sir. I tend to watch baseball or hockey."

"Call me Robert. I bought a racing team when I retired from the company," Robert informed him, and Ion could see the excitement shine in the man's face.

"Tell me about it."

Both Adrien and his mother rolled their eyes, but Ion didn't care. He'd found that the best way to truly get to know someone was to ask them about things they loved. Listening to Robert about his team was a small price to pay if it made Robert happy. That was what he planned to do with all of Adrien's family as he met them.

Chapter Eight

Ion nibbled on his nail, suddenly finding himself more nervous than he'd ever been. *Why did I think I could do this?* He paced the bedroom then paused in front of the mirror to check out his reflection. He tugged on the cuffs of his shirt, hoping he looked good enough to pass inspection for Alyssa's party. He'd never gone to a formal event like this, and he didn't want to embarrass Adrien or his family.

"Ion, can you come here for a moment," Adrien called from the living room area of the suite.

"Sure." He snatched up the small gift wrapped box he'd brought from the city.

As he entered the other room, Adrien turned around and Ion froze at the sight before him. The tuxedo Adrien wore had been tailored to fit him within an inch. His white shirt showed off his tan and his silk vest matched his eyes.

"What the hell am I doing here," Ion whispered.

Adrien snorted. "Honey, you're here to keep me from killing my family. I don't know how you've done it, but they love you. I've never seen any of them warm up to a person like they have to you. My mother hasn't made one comment about where your parents live or what they do. Amelia told me today that she wants to come visit us in the city, and they never come to Manhattan if they can help it."

Ion set Alyssa's present on the table by the door before he threw his arms around Adrien's neck. He brought his lover's lips down to his and devoured them. He poured all of his love and joy into their embrace. No matter how the party ended for him, he was so glad he'd gotten to know Adrien better.

After breaking their kiss, Adrien grinned. "Not that I'm complaining, Ion, but what was that for?"

"I love you," he blurted out then bit his lip.

Adrien looked a little stunned and Ion wasn't sure he wanted to know how Adrien felt about him.

"You don't have to answer me. I just wanted to let you know before we go down for the party. I hope I don't embarrass you," he muttered.

"God, you had to tell me this when I can't take you to bed to show you how much I love you," Adrien complained. "That's not fair."

"The party won't go on all night, love. Who says we can't sneak up here later on and have some fun before the end?" Ion nuzzled along Adrien's jaw.

Adrien moaned then eased Ion away from him. "You keep that up and we will be late, which is unforgivable to my mother. I called you in here to give you something."

He looked at the box Adrien held out to him. After opening it, he found a pair of sapphire cuff links. Ion lifted them out then held them up to the light.

"They're the same color as your eyes," he pointed out.

"I know. I thought you might like them. I figured Salvatore would include some with your tux, but I wanted to get you something." Adrien helped him switch the jewelry out.

Ion cradled Adrien's face in his hands. "Thank you."

He wasn't going to argue about Adrien buying him anything else. At least not the cuff links. They were a gift given not because Adrien thought Ion might not have the *right* kind, but because he simply wanted to give him something.

"You're welcome." Adrien kissed him quickly then motioned toward the door. "We should be getting down there."

"All right." Ion picked up Alyssa's present before following Adrien out of their suite.

The rest of the family had gathered in Robert's study for a quiet drink before the chaos of the party started. Ion hung back as Adrien went to greet his parents and Amelia. When he saw all of them standing there together in their finest clothes, he couldn't believe how beautiful the entire family was.

"It's stunning, isn't it?"

He turned to see Jonathon standing next to him, staring at the same sight he was. "Yes. I don't think it should be legal for them all to look so good."

Jonathon chuckled. "And you haven't even met the most beautiful of them all. Alain is almost angelic in looks. Too bad he's pure devil in his soul."

"He's not coming?" Ion hadn't asked Adrien about what members of his family were going to be there.

"Oh no. I'm sure there's a woman to be seduced, a horse to bet on, or a card game to be played somewhere in the world. His mother's birthday won't even be a thought in his head tonight." Jonathon sipped his whiskey then continued, "But Alyssa will forgive him when he chooses to appear because he knows how to wrap her around his finger."

Ion sort of understood what that was like, considering how his parents felt about Bogdan, but he had a feeling Alain was a whole lot worse than his older brother ever thought of being.

"Ion, you look quite handsome tonight." Alyssa gave him an air kiss before she spotted the box in his hand. "Oh, is that for me?"

He held it out. "Of course, you're the only birthday girl in the room."

"You didn't have to get me anything. It's enough that you chose to come with Adrien. I'm sure you heard horror stories about us." She winked while taking the gift.

He chuckled. "We've exchanged family horror stories, Alyssa. I'm happy to say you're all not nearly as bad as Adrien said you would be."

"We all know what he says about us," Amelia said as she joined their little group. "It's not flattering, but we say bad things about him all the time. It's the family tradition."

"I always thought he never brought a boyfriend home to meet us because he was embarrassed by us, but now I think he didn't bring one because he was ashamed of them." Robert clapped his hand to Ion's shoulder. "You should be proud. Adrien brought you here, so that must mean he thinks you're a good man."

"He's right here," Adrien spoke up from where he stood near the door of the study.

Ion started to say something, but Alyssa actually squealed when she opened Ion's present. Everyone stared at her in surprise, making Ion think it had been a while since she'd made that kind of sound.

"Oh my God, how did you know?" She lifted a long gold chain from the box, and the butterfly pendant dangled from it.

"Just a lucky guess." He owed Patrick big time for helping him out with what to buy.

"It's gorgeous." She gestured for Robert to put it on her. "I've been wanting one of these for months. But the designer was always so busy."

"As luck would have it, I know the designer and she was more than happy to make one for you." Once he'd spilled his guts to Patrice and explained why the necklace was so important to him.

Amelia and Jonathon admired the jewelry along with Robert while Adrien strolled over to Ion.

"You know someone who makes designer jewelry that costs thousands of dollars?" Adrien shot him a questioning glance.

Ion smirked. "Patrick's twin sister."

"Ah. That's not really fair you know. You're making the rest of us look bad." He encircled Ion's waist. "It's a good thing I like you, or I'd be jealous of how much my mother seems to love you. The only other person she's like this with is Alain."

"Jonathon was telling me about him. I'm not sure I want to meet your brother." Ion shifted to rest more of his weight on Adrien, trusting his lover to keep him standing.

"Don't worry. You won't be any time soon. I doubt he wants to come back here. Not enough excitement." Adrien brushed his lips over Ion's temple.

Mason cleared his throat. "Your guests will be arriving any minute now, Mrs Bellamy."

"Thank you, Mason." Alyssa gathered them all with a smile. "Are we ready to have fun tonight?"

"Yes," they all answered.

Adrien held Ion back as the rest filtered out of the room toward the foyer where they would gather to greet the people arriving. He looked at Adrien.

"What's up?"

"You know for the first time, I really am looking forward to tonight. I get to introduce people to the man I love. I'm going to be attending one of these parties with an intelligent man who who's going to help me see the world in a whole new light." Adrien rested his forehead against Ion's. "You've already made me see that my family isn't as terrible as I thought they were."

Ion rubbed his cheek on Adrien's. "Your family has been marvelous. They managed to raise you without too much damage done."

"Adrien, your mother is requesting your presence," Mason informed them.

Entwining their fingers, Ion took a step toward the door. "Let's go have some fun with your family, Adrien. But just remember. You get to meet mine and I don't think it's going to go nearly as smoothly."

Adrien's laughter warmed Ion's heart, and as they wandered down the hall to where the others were, Ion realized that loving Adrien removed the empty spaces he hadn't even known existed in his soul.

CLOSE THE
DISTANCE

Dedication

Being poor doesn't always mean not having money.
Sometimes it means not having love in your life.

Chapter One

"Do we have everything?"

Ion turned to look at Adrien as he wandered through their suite of rooms. "I think so, but if we don't, it's not like your mom can't send them back to the city for us."

Adrien frowned. "You're right. I just feel like I'm forgetting something."

Reaching out, Ion snagged Adrien then pulled him close, encircling his waist. He tugged on the blue silk tie his lover wore. "I told you not to get dressed up to meet my parents."

"What do you mean?" Adrien glanced down at his white linen dress shirt, tie and tailored black pants. "This isn't dressed up."

For him, it wasn't dressed up. Not when the man wore thousand dollar suits to the office every day. For Ion's family, a tie like that was for church, weddings and funerals. He trailed his fingers through the curls at the nape of Adrien's neck before taking the tie in hand to remove it.

"Trust me. You don't need a tie for dinner." He tossed it onto the bed then pressed open-mouthed kisses along Adrien's jaw. "I'd suggest you change your whole outfit, but I don't think you'd feel comfortable in anything else."

"I do have jeans and T-shirts, Ion," Adrien commented as he tipped his head, giving Ion more access to his neck. "I thought I'd try to make a good impression on them during our first meeting."

Ion hummed, not interested in talking about his parents anymore. He brought their lips together while he started to unbutton Adrien's shirt. Once he got it off, Ion let it drop to the floor then bent to lick one of the flat copper nipples covered with sparse hair.

Adrien cradled the back of his head, keeping him close. "We don't have time for this. Not if we want to get to your parents' before dinner."

"I'm not worried about that. We can go next Sunday or the week after that," he murmured, moving from one nipple to the other, sucking on it and using a little teeth. Ion worried the nub of flesh and drew a moan from Adrien.

He encouraged Adrien to ease back and, step by step, he moved them to the edge of the bed then he shoved. Laughing, he watched as Adrien tilted until he fell on the mattress.

"What the hell?" Adrien braced his hands on the comforter as he stared up at Ion.

"I'm feeling a little hungry," Ion muttered before dropping to his knees. He unbuckled Adrien's belt, fumbled with his zipper to get those crazy-expensive slacks open.

He tugged the fabric down while Adrien lifted his hips and his cock sprang out, hard and curved over his abs. Licking his lips, Ion studied the well-formed erection in front of him. Thicker and a little longer than his. The head was fleshy and purple and was shiny from pre-cum. It rose from a trimmed nest of dark curls and his balls hung heavy beneath it. Ion reached out to take them in hand. He fondled then rolled them in his fingers. Leaning in, he sucked one then the other. There was a salty taste to his skin along with the lingering scent of the soap they'd used earlier in the shower.

He pressed his tongue against the lightly furred sac before letting it slip from his mouth. Adrien gripped his head then directed his mouth to the tip of his shaft. Ion willingly opened, taking him without hesitation. He loved how it felt lying on his tongue.

When Adrien hit the back of his throat, Ion swallowed, massaging his length. His lover moaned and he smiled around the dick in his mouth. He loved knowing he could draw those sounds out and make Adrien lose control. After slipping his finger in beside Adrien's cock, he got it wet then rubbed it over Adrien's hole.

"Your mouth," Adrien murmured. "I love the way it feels. Almost as good as your ass."

Ion pushed just the tip of his finger inside and Adrien moaned. Arching, Adrien thrust into his mouth then impaled himself. It was what Ion wanted, his lover taking what he needed.

When they got back to the city, they were going to get tested. Once their negative results came back, he would finally get to feel what fucking bareback was like. Well, he'd get a chance to remember what it felt like. His first couple of times having sex had been non-condom times, and he'd been lucky not to catch anything.

One of his close friends had gotten HIV, and it had shaken Ion to his core. That was when he'd promised himself that he was never going to believe he was invincible again. He always carried condoms in his wallet.

But now, loving Adrien meant he could get rid of them and experience the amazing sensation of Adrien spilling inside him. A little tug on his hair brought his mind back to what he was doing. Ion went back to bobbing up and down, applying as much pressure as he could to draw another groan from Adrien.

He had two fingers inside Adrien and Ion twisted them to nail his gland. He gagged slightly when Adrien shoved his cock a little deeper than was comfortable for Ion. But he didn't back off, working Adrien as best he could until he got a tap on the cheek, letting him know Adrien was close.

He upped the pressure and movement until Adrien tensed under him, and his mouth was flooded with salty bitterness. Drinking it down, Ion tried to get all of it.

When Adrien began to soften, Ion licked him clean then let him slide out. Adrien pulled him up before encouraging him to lean forward. Adrien lapped at the cum on Ion's chin while working Ion's jeans open.

"Oh, fuck me," Ion whispered as the smooth skin of Adrien's hand surrounded his heated flesh.

He was primed, so it only took three hard tugs and he climaxed, coating Adrien's hand and his own pants. Working his cock, Adrien didn't let up until Ion was so sensitive, he had to get away from his lover. After rolling to one side, Ion stared up at the ceiling while he tried to get his breathing under control.

"Do you think we'll be able to get to your parents' on time?" Adrien asked a few minutes later.

Ion chuckled. "I guess we can try, or I can call Mom and let her know we'll be there next week. I'm just not sure what excuse I can give her, since usually I have to be on my death bed for her to let me off."

A knock on the door brought a frown to Adrien's face and they scrambled to get their clothes straightened. Ion grimaced at the mess he'd made in his underwear and jeans.

"I'm going to change. You answer that."

Adrien left the bedroom and Ion pushed the door almost shut so he could hear what was going on in the living room of the suite, but no one could see him pulling on a clean pair of pants.

"Mrs Bellamy needs you to attend her in the drawing room, sir," Mason told Adrien.

"What's wrong? Mother knows we have to leave for the city soon."

Ion didn't bother with underwear, just got his pants on as quickly as possible. Once he got everything situated and his shoes back on, he joined them.

"I'm not sure, sir. Your mother didn't confide in me, but I do know she received a phone call from your brother." Mason frowned at Ion when he walked into the room.

Adrien shook his head. "God damn it. If anyone can ruin a good day, it would be him. I wonder what kind of trouble he got into now."

"Tell you what, I'll call a cab, and head back to the city. If I leave now and call my mom, she'll delay dinner long enough for me to get there." Ion encircled Adrien's waist then placing a kiss on his cheek. "I know you're going to have to deal with this, if only to comfort your mother."

"I wish he'd grow up, Ion. This drives me crazy." Frustration deepened Adrien's voice then he sighed. "I'm sorry, Ion. I did want to meet them."

Ion grinned. "Don't be in such a hurry to get into that situation, love. I don't have much faith that my family will react the same way yours did."

"Still. It doesn't seem very fair that you had to endure dinner and a party, then I get out of it because of my brother."

Turning to look at Mason, Ion said, "Tell Alyssa that Adrien will be there in a few minutes."

"Yes, sir." Mason inclined his head to both of them before leaving.

Ion took Adrien's hand then led him to the couch where he sat, tugging him down. He cradled Adrien's face, holding him so he could gaze into his eyes. "You'll eventually get a chance to meet my family. We aren't breaking up any time soon. I love you, Adrien, and I can wait. You have to take care of your family first or at least, you have to ease your mother's mind, even if you want to let your brother twist in the wind."

Adrien leaned forward to rest his forehead against Ion's. "I'm tired of being the one to clean up his messes. Just once I would love it if he tried to fix his problems without calling Mother or me."

Embracing him, Ion pressed his lips against Adrien's ear. "Someday he will. Unfortunately, until then, you have to be the adult and help him out."

"I know. All right. I'll have Daniel drop you off at your parents'. If you want, he can take you back to your apartment afterwards as well." Adrien stood, taking Ion with him.

"I can grab the subway back. Daniel can either go home or come back to drive you to the city." He snagged his jacket from where he'd tossed it earlier then got his bag.

After wandering downstairs, Ion gave Mason his luggage to put in the trunk of the car. Ion thanked the man then followed Adrien to the drawing room where Alyssa waited.

Alyssa greeted him with a worried smile. "I hope you don't mind me stealing Adrien away from you, Ion."

He took her hand in his then covered it with his other one. "I don't mind at all, Alyssa. I completely understand. I have to head back, but I wanted to thank you for the wonderful weekend. I truly enjoyed meeting you and all of Adrien's family."

"I'm so glad Adrien brought you. You're the perfect match for him, and I look forward to seeing you again." She kissed his cheek and pressed his hand before letting him go. "Adrien, walk Ion out. This can wait until you say goodbye."

"Certainly, Mother." Adrien gestured for Ion to head out in front of him.

Daniel was standing by the car outside, and Ion pointed toward the man as they left the house. He turned back to kiss Adrien goodbye.

"I'll text you when I get to my parents'. Let me know if you're going to be back tonight or if you'll have to stay out here longer," he said.

Adrien nodded. "Of course. I'll see you tomorrow at work if I get all of this taken care of tonight."

Ion hugged him tight before strolling over to where Daniel held the door to the back of the car open. "Can you just drop me off at my parents'? Then you can go home or back here if necessary."

"Yes, sir." Daniel shut the door.

Leaning back in the leather seat, Ion pulled out his phone while Daniel climbed behind the wheel then started the vehicle. He dialed his parents' home number.

"Vasile residence. How may I help you?" his mother answered.

"Hey, Mama," he said, staring out of the window, watching the Bellamy mansion slowly fading out of sight.

"Ion. You are still coming to dinner tonight?"

It was funny that the first thought on her mind was dinner. "Yes. I'll be there, but not until six-thirty. I'm heading back into the city now."

She hummed and he could almost see her eyes narrow in suspicion. "Into the city? Where were you?"

"I was out in the Hamptons with my boyfriend, visiting his family." Ion braced for her reaction. "He was going to come and meet you tonight, but he had an emergency to take care of. He'll come out next Sunday, if it's all right with you."

Silence met his comment, not surprising him. Ion chose to wait her out because he wasn't going to let her off the hook. He waited to hear what she had to say.

"We'll talk about it when you get here. I'll let the others know that dinner will be a little late. Drive safe." She hung up without saying goodbye.

Ion tossed his phone onto his jacket in the seat next to him. He should've known Adrien wouldn't get a warm welcome at his home. His parents were nice people, but they were old-fashioned in their beliefs, which meant they thought he should marry a good girl and have children to continue the family name.

Bogdan had done his job, having married Olive and had two kids. Ion was a constant disappointment to his mother for not giving her more grandchildren to spoil and another daughter-in-law to teach to cook traditional family favorites. There was nothing to say that she couldn't teach Adrien to make them, and Ion wouldn't have been surprised if he wanted to learn.

He'd been taking a chance in bringing Adrien home, but he had wanted to give them a chance to meet the man he loved. Ion knew that if they turned their back on Adrien and refused him entrance to their home and family, Ion would choose Adrien over them. Life was too short to be miserable. He wouldn't deny the love he thought he could find with Adrien just because his parents didn't want him to be gay.

His phone rang and he checked the screen. It was his brother and he took a second to decide whether he wanted to deal with him at the moment. Finally, taking a deep breath, he answered, "Hello, Bogdan."

"What did you say to Mama?" No hello. Just immediate accusation.

"I told her I'd be late because I just left the Hamptons and was driving back in." He wanted to see what she'd told them.

"What's this about you spending the weekend with your boyfriend? And that he was going to come to dinner with you." Bogdan's unhappiness could be heard in his voice.

Ion rolled his eyes. "Yes. I spent the weekend with Adrien and his family. It was his mother's birthday and they had a party for her. I had planned on leaving early enough to get to dinner on time, but I didn't. Plus Adrien had some family business come up, so he couldn't make it."

"Don't you think you should've asked Mama and Pops before you just showed up with him?"

"Why would I? You didn't when you brought Olive home. Shouldn't I get the same consideration when I want to bring my boyfriend home?" Ion was starting to get angry. He might have expected such a reaction, but that didn't mean he had to like it.

Bogdan snorted. "Not when you know how they feel about your life style choices, Ion."

Ion growled. "My choices? Do you think I'd choose this lifestyle? That I do this because I want to upset our parents? Thank you so much for judging and condemning me for something I have no control over."

His brother started to say something, but Ion interrupted, "Never mind. Tell Mama I'm sorry, but I won't be coming for dinner tonight. I've suddenly lost my appetite."

He hung up then tossed his phone away. When it rang a few seconds later, he just let it go to voicemail. He wasn't interested in listening to his brother tell him why he needed to cut his parents some slack. He'd been doing that ever since he'd come out and had to listen to his mother talk about some nice girl she'd met at the grocery store or somewhere else in the neighborhood.

After spending the weekend with Adrien's family, who didn't seem to care that he was a guy or that he came from a blue-collar family, it hurt to know his couldn't be as understanding. The Bellamys liked him for himself, and because Adrien liked him. Why couldn't his family be the same way?

"Daniel, there's been a change of plans. I need you to take me to my place. I'm not going to my parents," he informed his driver.

"Certainly, sir." Daniel didn't ask for directions, so Ion trusted him to know where to go.

Leaning back, Ion closed his eyes. He'd call Adrien later to let him know what had happened, not wanting to bother him when there was nothing he could do about it. At least he'd be able to get his homework done early instead of having to stay up late to work on it.

Chapter Two

Adrien returned to the drawing room after he watched the car disappear down the driveway. His mother stood by a window that overlooked the backyard. She played with the necklace Ion had given her, running it back and forth on the chain.

"I'm sorry to keep you from going with Ion," she said as Adrien joined her.

He touched her shoulder. "Ion understands that family is important, and to be honest, I don't think he's all that thrilled to have me meet his parents. So you've given him a reprieve."

His mother glanced at him. "Why wouldn't he want you to meet his parents? Is he ashamed of you or something?"

Her indignation made him laugh, as did her belief that Ion would ever be ashamed of him. "No. Ion isn't ashamed of me. The problem lies in the fact that I'm a guy, not a girl, and more than likely if they find out that I now own the company they work for, that'll be a problem as well."

"Why?" Alyssa wandered back to the loveseat then sat. She gestured toward the chair across from her. "I don't know why either one would be an issue."

After sitting, he stared at her for a moment then said, "I'm sorry, Mother. I seriously underestimated you and the rest of my family."

She smiled. "You don't have to apologize, honey, but I'm not surprised. You've been thinking we're a bunch of snobs for a while now. And yes, we haven't done much to change your opinion of us, and God knows, your brother continues to prove you right in that respect."

"Let's discuss what Alain's done now." Adrien changed the subject, not wanting to talk about what he'd thought. It would take a little while to get his mind wrapped around how wrong he'd been.

Alyssa sighed. "He called to ask if I would send him some money. He seems to have gone through the allowance you give him each month."

"Already?" Adrien shook his head. "I just had that transferred into his account on Friday."

"I know. He didn't tell me what he did with the money and, frankly, I'm too scared to ask. I'm afraid he'll tell me he's addicted to drugs or something." Her worry showed on her face.

Adrien stood then went to sit next to her on the couch. He took her hand in his. "Mother, you need to cut the apron strings and I have to cut the purse strings. We've been enabling him to keep doing what he does, not that I know what that is. I get bills from hotels and casinos, so I assume he's gambling."

Alyssa sighed. "I know I spoil him and let him get away with things you and Amelia never did, but he had such a hard start and I didn't want him to have to struggle for the rest of his life."

"I know, but he needs to grow up. None of us can keep taking care of things for him. What happens if he out lives all of us? How is he going to take care of himself then?" As angry as Adrien got with Alain, he didn't like cutting him off either, but he knew they had to do something to get his little brother to accept responsibility for his own actions.

"Maybe you could cut his allowance. Don't take it all away from him, Adrien." She squeezed his hand. "Tell him he has to come home. That you want to see him and talk about what is going on. Maybe give him a job at the company. Your father never took him seriously."

He thought about what she said. It was true. The moment Adrien was born it had been assumed he would take over the company when Robert was ready to retire. Amelia had been expected to marry well, have children and do charity work like her mother. There had been no expectations for Alain, as long as he didn't embarrass the family name. To tell the truth, Alain had done a very good job keeping the Bellamy name out of the gossip rags, for the most part.

Hell, Adrien had been in them more than Alain had. How had that happened? Had Adrien paying off hotels and casinos kept people from talking, or was Alain smarter than any of them gave him credit for?

"I think you might be on to something, Mother. I'll cut his allowance in half with the caveat that he has to come to New York and see me face-to-face. I haven't talked to him in over a year and it's time for a family chat." He grimaced then said, "I might be able to find him a job in the company, if he convinces me that's what he wants."

His mother laughed. "I'm pretty sure Alain will say he's fine and doesn't need anything so mundane as a job."

"Probably not, but I have to make the offer. I'll expect him to seriously think about it because I don't plan on funding his jet-setting journey around the world for much longer." He brushed a kiss over his mother's cheek before he stood. "I'm going to try and get a hold of Alain. I'll see if I can get him home soon."

Alyssa stood then threw her arms around him. He was a little surprised because his family wasn't into public displays of affection, even in the privacy of their own homes. He hugged her back, breathing in her familiar scent of Chanel No. 5.

When they broke apart, she looked up at him. "I'm proud of you, Adrien. You've become an amazing man. We all ask so much of you to keep the company going and help your family when we need it. I'm glad that you found Ion. He's perfect for you."

"We haven't been together that long, Mother. Don't be picking out wedding venues yet." He winked and she giggled.

As he left the room, she called out, "There's no need to look for a venue, dear. You'll get married here, of course."

Waving at her, he went to find Mason to see if the butler knew where his father was. He found Mason in the kitchen talking to one of the maids. After getting Mason's attention, he waited in the hallway until he came to him.

"How may I help you, sir?"

"I wonder if you know where my father is?" Adrien asked.

Mason nodded. "He's out in the garage. If you hurry, you should be able to catch him before he leaves. He goes to the club on Sunday afternoons."

"Thanks." Adrien strolled to the garage and got there just as his father was about to climb into his car. "Father," he called.

"Adrien?" Robert looked at him. "What are you still doing here? I thought you and Ion had left a while ago."

"Mother needed to talk to me and now I need to talk to you."

Robert shut the car door then approached him. "It was about your brother, right?"

Adrien led the way back into the house. Once there, he went to his father's study where he sat on a chair and his father took his seat behind the desk. Robert sighed before he waved a hand in Adrien's direction.

"Tell me what's going on now."

He gave his father the rundown of what his mother had told him, plus his decision to cut Alain's allowance in half and call his brother home. "Mother suggested I offer him a job in the company. What do you think of that?"

Robert rubbed his chin while he thought and Adrien stayed quiet. He'd learned patience while dealing with his father. Robert Bellamy didn't rush a decision—he worked out as many angles as possible in his mind before giving voice to any idea.

"You can certainly give it a try. I'm not sure Alain is reliable enough to be counted on for any important job, but there must be something. We own several companies and corporations. Something will show up that will fit his personality."

Adrien nodded. "Thanks. I appreciate the input. I'll have Sidney go through our different assets and see if there's anything that will work."

Robert stood. "If that's all, I'm on my way to the club. Call me tomorrow."

They shook hands, and Adrien watched his father leave as he pulled out his phone. He wasn't looking forward to the conversation he was about to have, but like his parents, he realized it had to be done. Everyone had given Alain a great deal of leeway to go about his business without consequence. Well, the leash was about to get much shorter and he knew Alain wasn't going to like it at all.

He dialed Alain's number before walking over to the French doors leading out onto the verandah. Once there, he sat at the small wicker table his mother often had breakfast at. Staring out over the beach and water, he wished Ion was there. He had a feeling he was going to need to hear a friendly voice after he was finished with Alain.

"Hey, Adrien." Alain sounded rushed.

"Hello, Alain. Do you have time to talk?" As much as he knew the conversation had to happen, Adrien wasn't going to interrupt anything his brother was doing.

Alain's laugh was strained. "Not at the moment. Can I call you back in an hour?"

Adrien wanted to say no, but he was willing to give Alain a little more playtime before he got yanked back home. "Sure. Please do call me back. It's extremely important."

"I will. I wanted to talk to you as well." Alain hung up before Adrien could react to that statement.

After setting the phone on the table, he leaned back in the chair. He steepled his fingers then pressed them against his lips as he thought. *What can Alain possibly want to talk to me about?* Alain rarely called him, not even for money. Usually when he needed something, he'd call their mother and she'd contact Adrien.

He picked up his phone then sent Ion a text.

How's dinner going?

It vibrated in his hand when he received Ion's text. He frowned when he read what Ion told him.

Wouldn't know. Didn't end up going.

Adrien didn't like the sound of that.

What happened?

I don't want to talk about it in a text.

He understood that.

I'll be back tonight. Can I come over or maybe you could meet me at my place?

It took a while before Ion answered him.

Your place. I'll bring stuff to spend the night.

Great. Just let yourself in. I'll let you know when I leave here. Love you.

Love you too.

Returning the phone to the table, he shook his head. The day was starting to turn out far more complicated than he'd thought it would when he'd woken up that morning. He just hoped he could help Ion with his problem, because he had a feeling that the solution he'd come up with for his brother was going to be a battle.

"Sir, would you like a drink or something?" Mason stepped out onto the verandah.

"Yes, I'd love some coffee, please." After standing, Adrien stuffed his phone in his pocket. "Just set it on the table. I'll be back in a few minutes."

"Certainly." Mason inclined his head slightly before going back into the house.

Adrien wandered through the gardens to the beach where he walked along the edge of sand and the water. One weekend, he and Ion would have to take his sailboat out for a trip down the coast. Maybe he could convince Ion to take a week off then they could go all the way down to the Outer Banks or Charleston.

After walking for about ten minutes and trying to relax, he returned to the table where he found a carafe of coffee and a cup. He poured it out before sitting. He'd just taken a sip when his phone rang. Swallowing quickly, Adrien retrieved his phone and answered.

"Bellamy."

"Hey, big bro. Are you somewhere you can talk?" Alain's voice was upbeat, yet Adrien heard a hint of worry in it.

"I happen to be on the verandah at Mother and Father's. It was Mother's birthday yesterday and I came out to celebrate it with her."

"Oh fuck. God damn it. And I didn't even remember to wish her a happy birthday this morning when I called." Alain growled under his breath.

"She'll forgive you, but I suggest you call her as soon as we get done talking. That way you won't have to grovel too much." Adrien fidgeted with his cup. "What did you want to talk to me about?"

Alain sighed. "I'm going to be in New York on Wednesday, and I wanted to know if we could meet up. What I need to discuss with you can't be talked about over an open phone line like this."

An open phone line? Sounds like spy talk. He cleared his throat. "Yes, well, I'll make sure my schedule is clear. Maybe we could meet for lunch at my place. That way what we have to say to each other doesn't bother anyone else." Adrien smiled when Alain laughed.

"Probably a good idea. I know you think I'm a worthless ass who blows through his allowance, spending it on women, drugs and gambling."

He started to protest then closed his mouth. If he was honest, that really was what he thought about his brother. He'd just never imagined Alain would acknowledge it.

"And in some ways you're right about me. There are other things I'm involved in that I need to talk to you about. You need to be read into the situation in case something happens."

"Read in? You're starting to sound like those spy shows Mother likes to watch." Adrien shook his head. "You better not be into anything dangerous, Alain. Mother would lose her mind if you were hurt. She loves you best, you know."

Alain chuckled. "I know, and I admit to using that love to my advantage from time to time. I have to go now, Adrien. I'll text you when I get to the city on Wednesday."

"Fine. Do you need money right now?" As much as he wanted to say no, he'd give Alain the cash if he were in trouble.

"No." Alain huffed in annoyance. "I'm fine at the moment. I have enough to pay for stuff until I get in."

Adrien relaxed a little. "All right. Call Mother soon. Take care, brother."

"You too. Oh and congratulations on the new boyfriend. Mother was suitably impressed with him. So he must be a good one." Alain hung up before Adrien could reply.

He finished his coffee before cleaning up. After carrying the tray to the kitchen, he went to find his mother. She was in the Pink Room, which she had claimed as her own office at the house—it was where she did all the paperwork for the charities on whose boards she served.

Checking to make sure she wasn't on the phone, he found her typing on her keyboard while peering at the computer screen.

"You know, you should go and get reading glasses at least. If you wore them here, no one would comment on them." He grinned as she glared at him. "Father would still love you even if you wore glasses."

"Hush." She gestured toward a chair. "Did you talk to Alain?"

"Yes. He should be calling you again soon. But I didn't talk to him about the cut in his allowance or the job. He's coming to New York on Wednesday and wants to meet with me. I thought I'd talk to him about it then."

Her face lit up. "Alain's coming home?"

Adrien hated bursting her happy bubble. "I don't know if he planned on stopping by to visit you and Father. You'll have to ask him about that. I just know he'll be in the city and wants to talk to me. I figured it would be the best time to discuss his allowance and things then."

Frowning, she leaned back in her chair. "Why would he come without visiting? How much trouble is he in, Adrien?"

"I don't know. He didn't say anything about that. Just that he wanted to talk. I assume if he were in trouble, he would've let you know. I even asked if he needed more money and he said he was fine."

He didn't have to explain how odd it was, though he'd only admit to himself that it worried him. Alain wasn't acting like the selfish prick he usually was, and Adrien wasn't sure how to deal with it.

Her eyebrows shot up and she looked concerned. "I'll see if I can get him to tell me what's going on. I just hope he hasn't upset anyone dangerous."

Was it strange that both of them had come to that conclusion independently of each other? Of course, with as much gambling as Alain seemed to be doing, getting on the wrong side of a certain kind of people wouldn't come as a surprise. His brother was the type of guy who would ask for help if he needed it. Hell, he'd never been shy about that.

"I don't think he has, Mother. You know he'd have said something to us if he had." Adrien sighed then stood. "I'm going to head home then, since you have everything in hand. I'll call you tomorrow."

His mother lifted her chin so he could place a kiss on her cheek. "Good. If Alain approves, your father and I will come in and we'll all go to dinner on Wednesday. Will Ion be able to come with us?"

"I'll have to check with him. He might have class that night."

"You find out and let me know. I assume you'll be bringing him down more often, so I'll be seeing him again." She smiled and Adrien laughed as he left.

"Daniel hasn't arrived back, sir," Mason informed him as he appeared in the hallway.

"I know. I told him to drop my bags off at my apartment then just go home for the night. Father won't mind if I take one of the cars. Daniel can bring it back tomorrow, or Father can pick it up during the week." Adrien grabbed a set of keys from where they were hanging by the garage door.

Mason lifted the corner of his mouth in a slight smile. "I'll let him know. It was good to see you, sir, and to meet Mr Vasile."

Adrien clapped Mason on the shoulder. "Thank you, Mason. I'm sure you'll be seeing more of him from now on."

"Wonderful, sir. Drive safely."

He picked one of the sedans his father had purchased for his mother to drive if she was so inclined. It had been several years since she had driven herself anywhere, so he knew they wouldn't miss it. When he turned it on, he shivered at the well-tuned purr of the engine. It might not get used very often, but his father made sure all of the cars were taken care of.

After he got the radio on the station he wanted to listen to, he pulled out of the garage then drove to the road. As much as he enjoyed having Daniel drive him places, there were times he liked being behind the wheel and in control of his own direction.

Usually he took his time driving back from the Hamptons, but he wanted to see Ion and hold him. Maybe even find out what had gone wrong with dinner.

Chapter Three

Ion glanced up when he heard a key in the door then he stood to make his way to the foyer, where Adrien was tossing his keys into the bowl on the table.

"You drove yourself?" He leaned on the doorframe, crossing his arms over his chest as he watched Adrien hang up his jacket.

"Daniel hadn't made it back yet, and I didn't want to wait around for him." Adrien approached him to wrap his arms around Ion's waist. "After getting your text about you not going to your parents, I wanted to get home to see you."

Grimacing, Ion encircled Adrien's shoulders before resting his forehead against Adrien's. "I knew it wasn't going to go well, so I shouldn't have been upset about it."

"Let's go in the bedroom," Adrien suggested as he stepped back.

Ion held on to Adrien's hand while they strolled to the bedroom. Once they were lying on the comforter, he curled up into Adrien's side, happy to have him there.

"Do you want to tell me about it?" Adrien ran his hand up and down Ion's arm.

"There's not much to tell. I was on my way to my parents' and I called my mom to let her know that I'd be late." He closed his eyes while breathing in Adrien's familiar scent.

Adrien hummed, but didn't say anything and Ion nuzzled closer.

"I told her that I had been in the Hamptons with my boyfriend and that was why I would be late. I informed her that you wouldn't be able to come with me because of family issues. She didn't say much. Just said we'd talk about it when I got there."

He brushed a kiss over the underneath of Adrien's jaw.

"She hung up on me. A minute or two later my brother called to interrogate me. He wanted to know why Mama was crying and all upset. I explained how I was going to bring you to dinner, but that you couldn't come this time. He asked why I had to do that. Why couldn't I just come to dinner without you? I should respect their beliefs and traditions."

"Traditions?" Adrien eased over until he lay on his back with Ion covering him like a blanket. Ion began to unbutton his shirt, but it was obvious Adrien wanted to know the rest of the story.

"That marriage should be one man and one woman. I'll be turned straight by the love of the right woman." Ion snorted. "They don't understand that it's not a choice. I was born gay, yet they think I'm choosing to be this way to make their lives difficult. I think my brother leans that way as well."

Adrien untucked Ion's T-shirt from his jeans then ran his fingers over the small of his back. Ion shuddered, absorbing the warm, gentle care in his touch. He rocked against Adrien's groin then groaned as Adrien grabbed his ass to press them tight together.

"You ended up not going then?"

Adrien sounded slightly breathless and Ion undulated again.

"No, I didn't and I don't plan on going until they can afford me the same courtesy as they do my brother and his wife. I'm their son. Shouldn't they love me no matter who I love? To be honest, as much as I'd love for them to accept us unconditionally, I'm willing to let it just be the fact that they won't ignore you exist. They don't have to be comfortable with us, but you should to be able to come to dinner without comments or you being ignored. If they can't do that, then I'm not going to dinner."

He crushed their lips together, not wanting to talk about it anymore. Maybe he would change his mind in the next day or so when the anger and hurt faded a little. Adrien opened to him, letting Ion take control of how deep the kiss went. He swept his tongue in, running it over Adrien's teeth.

Adrien sucked on him for a second then let him go. Easing down, Ion trailed kisses along the line of Adrien's throat to his chest. He got his shirt unbuttoned and shoved apart so he could continue licking and sucking. Humming softly, he pinched one of Adrien's nipples between his thumb and finger to give it a little twist.

"Oh, fuck." Adrien groaned, threading his fingers into Ion's hair. He didn't seem interested in trying to take control. Just held Ion's head gently.

Ion kept playing with the nub while he took the other in his mouth. Flicking it with his tongue, he felt Adrien jerk. Moving between the two, he played with them until they were red and probably ached. When he finished, he licked and nipped his way down to dip his tongue into Adrien's belly button.

Chuckling, Adrien tried to shift away, but Ion pressed on his hips to keep him still. When Adrien's cock hit his chin, he wiggled enough to lap at the flared head. He reached down to cup Adrien's balls then squeezed.

"Oh, God," Adrien muttered as he arched and Ion allowed more of his length to slip into his mouth.

Before it could go any further, Ion rose up onto his knees. "We need to change spots."

Adrien blinked at him and Ion knew his lover was having trouble making sense of what Ion had said. Instead of waiting, he shifted them so that he was on his back and Adrien straddled his head. He wrapped one hand around Adrien's shaft then positioned it at his mouth.

"Now fuck me," he ordered before opening his mouth to take Adrien in.

Adrien started thrusting in and Ion applied suction while getting two of his fingers wet. Once that happened, he slid them around to rub over Adrien's hole before pressing in.

As he moved between fingers and mouth, Adrien held onto the headboard and Ion encouraged him to thrust as deep as he wanted. When his cock hit the back of Ion's throat, he swallowed and Adrien yelled.

"Fuck! I'm coming."

Ion hummed, not worried about it. The first spurt warned him then Adrien's cum flooded his mouth. He drank it down as fast as he could, but some of it trickled from the corners of his lips.

The moment Adrien's softening penis fell from his lips, Ion urged him to reposition so that Ion's dick was at his opening. Ion reached for the bottle of lube he'd set on the bed but Adrien seemed to be in a hurry. Without waiting for Ion to get the condom on and slick up, Adrien began pushing back.

"Wait, love. I don't want you to hurt," Ion protested.

Adrien's grin seemed strained. "It'll be okay. We'll just take it slow. I don't need the lube."

Ion let the tube drop from his fingers before taking a hold of Adrien's hips. He didn't do anything except steady him while Adrien lowered himself. He winced as Adrien bit his bottom lip and wanted to stop him before he hurt himself.

But Adrien didn't stop, just kept going until Ion was buried as deep inside him as he could get. Ion stayed still for a moment then when Adrien clenched his muscles around him, he began to move.

Together, they undulated and rocked, and Ion tried to hit Adrien's gland every stroke in. He knew it wasn't going to take long for him to climax. Giving Adrien head had primed him to the point where he wouldn't last now that he was inside his lover.

He grunted when Adrien leaned down to lick the drying cum off his face then gasped when he sat up to take him even deeper. Their movements grew rougher and Ion surged up, flipping them over so that Adrien was under him. It gave him more leverage to pound Adrien's ass.

Adrien stared up at him and Ion got lost in them as he drove inside the man. Sweat dripped from his chin to pool on Adrien's chest while he fucked him. Grunts and the sound of skin hitting skin filled the room, building Ion's climax throughout his body. His balls drew tight and Ion threw back his head.

"Ah!" He yelled as he came, spilling into Adrien's ass.

When his arms gave out, he collapsed into Adrien's embrace. His chest heaved like bellows as he tried to calm down. Ion pressed his face where Adrien's neck and shoulder came together, flicking his tongue out to taste the beads of sweat that trailed down Adrien's throat.

Finally, he rolled to one side and Adrien winced as he slid out. Ion glared at him.

"See, that's why you should've waited for me to get the lube. Now you're going to be sore." He stroked his hand over Adrien's chest.

"Don't worry. I like being able to feel you every time I sit, or move for that matter." Adrien cradled his face. "I'm not fragile, honey. I can take getting my ass reamed by you."

Ion sighed before he climbed off the bed. "Let's go take a shower. We'll clean up then figure out what we're going to do for dinner, since I skipped out on mine."

Yawning, he held out his hand for Adrien to take and Adrien laughed when he took it.

"Maybe we should take a nap and get something to eat afterwards," Adrien suggested.

"Sounds like a plan to me."

After they showered and dried off, they changed the sheets on the bed before crawling in to snuggle close. Ion closed his eyes, letting his anger at his parents slide to the background. He'd deal with all of that later.

* * * *

Later on that night, Ion rested back against the couch and glanced over at Adrien. "How did the conversation with your brother go?"

Adrien looked up from his laptop where he'd been checking his emails. "It was kind of strange. He ended up calling me and asking that I meet him on Wednesday. He's coming to New York for some reason."

"Really? How long has it been since he's been here? I know you haven't seen him in a while." Ion rested his hand on Adrien's thigh.

"It's been over a year since I've seen him face-to-face. I wasn't able to make Mother's party last year because I was out of town on business. Today, I decided to cut his allowance in half and force him to take a job at the New York office. I never got to mention that to him."

Ion tightened his grip for a second then let go. "How do you think he'll react when you tell him that?"

Adrien shrugged. "I don't know. Probably not very happy, but my parents will support me, so I don't care how he reacts. The weird thing is, he said he had something to talk to me about, which is why he wants to meet. I can't imagine what he has to tell me."

"Maybe he got a girl pregnant and needs you to take care of it," Ion suggested as he picked up his coffee mug to take a sip.

"It could be, but to be honest, I've never got the feeling that Alain is that kind of guy. He's a gambler and a bit of a flake, yet he doesn't strike me as being that careless." Adrien shut his computer down then glanced at him. "And while I've seen pictures of him with tons of different women, I've always got the feeling he leans more in our direction than the straight side."

Ion shot Adrien a quick glance. "I guess I never noticed that. Just all those pictures of the women he escorted to parties and events. How could he hide something like being gay from the paparazzi?"

"How do any of the stars hide their secrets?" Adrien set his computer aside then stood. "Do you want some more coffee?"

"No. If I have any more, I won't be sleeping tonight."

As Adrien went into the kitchen, Ion's phone rang. He checked the screen and grinned. "Hey, Patrick."

"You're not at home," Patrick accused him.

"Umm…no. I'm over at Adrien's. Why?"

"I stopped by to see if you wanted to grab some dinner, but of course you weren't there." Patrick sounded upset.

Ion glanced up to see Adrien motion that he'd be in his study. Nodding, Ion leaned forward to brace his elbows on his knees.

"What's wrong?"

Patrick huffed and Ion could practically hear his annoyance. "Nothing really. Just haven't been in a good mood lately, and I feel like you've been more caught up in Adrien. Like you're forgetting me."

Ah…there was the real issue, and Ion understood how Patrick could think that. They hadn't done much together since Ion had started seeing Adrien.

"Patrick, you're my best friend and I'm never going to forget about you. Can you wait a sec?"

"Sure."

He set his phone down before going to Adrien. He found him reading some papers in his study.

"Would it be okay for Patrick to come over?" He leaned in the doorway to ask.

Adrien glanced up. "He's more than welcome to come over any time you want him over. You can consider this your place, Ion."

"Thanks." He blew him a kiss before heading back to his phone. "Patrick, why don't you come over to Adrien's? We'll have some ice cream and watch a movie or something."

"Mr Bellamy won't mind?" Patrick asked and Ion heard the curiosity in his friend's voice.

"He said you were more than welcome to come over. In fact, he said I should treat his apartment like it's my place." And it was right then that it hit Ion. "Holy shit!"

Patrick chuckled. "That just hit you, huh?"

"Yeah. Are you coming over?"

"Hell yeah. I want to see how the other half lives, and also your future place of residency. I'll pick up a carton of ice cream for us to share. Does Adrien want anything?"

"He'll have some ice cream with us if he wants anything." Ion flopped back into the cushions. "Just get your ass over here."

"All right. Text me his address and I'll be there as soon as I can." Patrick hung up.

Ion sent his friend Adrien's address then set his phone on the coffee table before he stood to go back to Adrien.

"Is Patrick coming over?" Adrien inquired when Ion entered the room.

"Yes. He's stopping to get ice cream on the way." Ion walked around the desk as Adrien pushed away from it so Ion could stand between his legs.

Adrien rested his hands on Ion's hips and looked up at him. "What do you want to ask me?"

"How do you know I want to ask you anything?" Ion ran his fingers through Adrien's hair.

"You just had this look on your face. Like you suddenly got thinking about something." Adrien

152

pressed his face to Ion's stomach. "Are you trying not to freak out that I told you to treat my place like it's yours?"

"Yes." Ion wasn't sure what he was thinking, except that it was a huge step.

Adrien kissed Ion's abs before he straightened up to look at him. "I'm not asking you to move in with me. At least not yet. I know we've been moving really fast and you might want to get to know me better before we decide if we want to live together."

Ion swallowed and Adrien grinned.

"I just want you to feel comfortable enough here that you wouldn't think twice about inviting any of your friends over. I know Patrick is probably starting to feel neglected because I've been monopolizing your time."

"Yeah. That's why I asked if he could come over. I don't want him to resent you because I love you and I'm not giving you up, but I don't want to give him up either." Ion bent down to kiss Adrien.

"I love you too, Ion. We're taking this a step at a time, and when we both feel it's right, we'll talk about our living situation. Though I have to ask you something."

"Sure." Ion braced his hands on the edge of the desk. "Ask away."

"I'm meeting Alain here on Wednesday and I know you're working during the day, but I wasn't sure if you had class or not."

Ion ran his schedule through his mind and nodded. "Yeah. I have class that night. So you don't have to feel bad about asking me not to come over then."

"It's not so much not coming over. I just wanted to let you know that I'd be busy all day and probably won't be able to see you that night. Well, I guess it depends on how long my meeting with Alain goes." Adrien frowned.

"I'm sure it will go fine. Of course, he'll probably be upset, but you have to do this or he'll never learn his lesson." Ion straightened then strolled toward the door. "You're more than welcome to join Patrick and me for ice cream and movies if you want."

Adrien snorted. "Maybe I will later. I need to go over the files Winston sent to me about that company."

"Okay. I'm going to throw a frozen pizza in the oven. I know we already ate, but we like to snack while we gossip."

"Can you put two in? I'll grab some of that." Adrien flipped open the file he had been reading when Ion came in.

"I'll let you know when it's done."

After putting the food in the oven, Ion got out a book out that he had to read for one of his classes. *Might as well get a head start on this week's homework.* He curled up on the couch to get comfortable.

The pizzas were ready to come out of the oven when Patrick knocked on the door. Ion glanced up to see Adrien making his way to let Patrick in. He set them on the counter to cool a little then went out to the foyer.

"Thanks for letting me come over, Mr Bellamy," Patrick said as he stepped in.

"Patrick, we're not at work, so you can call me Adrien. Besides you're making me feel like Ion's father, letting his friend come over to play." Adrien took Patrick's jacket from him then hung it up.

Ion took the bag Patrick held then led the way to the kitchen. "What kind did you get?"

"Superman of course." Patrick glanced around and his eyes lit up when he saw the pizzas. "I'm shocked he has frozen food of any kind. I would've thought he would only have, like, gourmet pizzas delivered from the best joints in the city."

"Usually I do, but sometimes I get hungry at two in the morning and don't want to order anything. So I throw one in." Adrien propped his shoulder against the doorframe.

They laughed when Patrick blushed, but Ion bumped his hip into Patrick's.

"See what happens when you assume. Now you get the wine open and poured. I'll cut them and Adrien, grab some plates."

Within minutes, Adrien was back in his study while Ion and Patrick were sitting on the leather couch, getting ready to watch the episode of *Sons of Anarchy* they had missed the week before.

Once the episode was over, Ion took their plates to the kitchen then dished out bowls of ice cream. He took one out to Patrick before taking the other one to Adrien.

"Here's dessert," he said as he walked in.

Adrien looked up from where he stood. He was on the phone so Ion mouthed an apology as he set the bowl on the desk. Adrien smiled at him then turned away. He went back to Patrick and they snuggled together on the couch while eating.

"So did you freak out a little when he told you to treat his apartment like it was yours?" Patrick poked him in the side.

Ion nodded. "A little. I mean, we've already said we loved each other and I realize that moving in together is a natural next step. I just wasn't ready to do it so soon."

"Did he ask you?" Patrick shot straight up on the couch to look at him. "And you've already told him you loved him?"

"No, he didn't ask me and yes, I've already told him that." Ion put his bowl on the table before facing Patrick. "I know it's fast, but why should I wait to tell him when it's how I feel? It's not going to change the longer I wait to do it. Besides, he loves me too. Hell, it's not like we're going out and getting married tomorrow."

"God, I'd hope not. I need to go get a new suit before I can stand up for you." Patrick grinned. "Besides, it'll be a big society wedding and you have to have some idea how crazy those can be."

"A big wedding?" Ion shook his head. "We aren't getting married."

"Not yet, but if he's already letting you call his place yours and telling you to invite whomever you want over, then I can see where this is heading." Patrick threw his hands in the air as he fell back against the couch. "I can just see it. It'll be a summer wedding and you'll both look dashing in your tuxedoes. You should totally have it in Central Park."

"If we ever decide to get married, the ceremony would be in my parents' back yard in the Hamptons," Adrien said as he strolled through the room to the kitchen.

"Oops," Patrick whispered behind his hand before bursting out in laughter.

Shaking his head, Ion rolled his eyes. *Great. Now Adrien thinks I'm going to want him to marry me. Yet now that the thought has been put out there, I kind of want to marry him. Spending the rest of my life with him would be awesome.*

Adrien wandered back in, another glass of wine in his hand, then stopped to brush a kiss over Ion's forehead. "I'm going to watch the news in the bedroom. I'll see you tomorrow, Patrick."

"Goodnight, sir." Patrick waited until Adrien was out of the room before he whirled to glare at Ion. "It's not fair."

"What isn't?" Ion muttered as he stared after Adrien, ogling his ass.

"He looks gorgeous in thousand dollar suits and ties. But in jeans and a T-shirt, the man is devastating." Patrick pouted. "I want one of my own."

Ion threw his arms around Patrick to hug him tight. "You'll find one. Why not try with Sidney?"

Patrick shook his head then buried his face in Ion's shoulder. "He's definitely not interested in me, and wouldn't be even if we didn't work together. I told you he's straight."

"How do you know for sure? Have you ever seen him dating anyone?" Ion frowned as he tried to remember seeing Sidney with a date at Alyssa's birthday party. But then he remembered he hadn't seen Sidney at all. Maybe the man hadn't come.

"I've seen pictures of him in the society pages and he always has some pretty blonde on his arm."

"That doesn't mean anything. He just might not be ready to come out yet." Ion didn't know why he was pushing Sidney at Patrick. While he didn't know the CFO of Bellamy International, he had a feeling the man wasn't what Patrick needed to make him happy.

Patrick pushed him away before snatching up his bowl. "I don't want to discuss this anymore. Tell me all about Mrs Bellamy's birthday bash. I bet it was amazing."

Ion let Patrick change the subject. They would circle around to it again some other night. "It was crazy, man. Oh, and she loved the necklace Patrice made for her."

He went on to describe everything, knowing Patrick did want to know all the details.

Chapter Four

Ion dropped his messenger bag on his chair before falling face first onto the couch. The week had been hard and it was only half over. Learning everything he needed to at Bellamy then going to class at night to learn everything else he could was exhausting. Yet he found he was enjoying it.

He'd seen Adrien a few times throughout the day, but neither of them went out of their way to hunt each other down. Mostly because they didn't want to make their relationship obvious, though Ion was sure that Adrien had told Sidney about it. The CFO kept eyeing him like he wasn't completely sure about the whole situation. Ion was going to prove that his promotion was deserved, and not because he was sleeping with the boss.

His phone rang and he dug it out from his bag. Without looking at it, he answered.

"Hello?"

"Ion."

Shit! It was his mother.

"Hello, Mama." He sat up then curled up into the corner of the couch. Wrapping his arm around his knees, he rested his forehead on them.

"Why didn't you come to supper last Sunday?"

"I decided not to come because I know you wouldn't be willing to treat Adrien like you do Olive." He took a deep breath.

She sighed. "We would be polite to him, Ion. He's your friend and your friends are always welcome at our table."

"He's more than a friend. He's the man I love and I want you to acknowledge that."

"You're not gay, so why do you insist on acting this way? Why are you so angry at me and your father that you would do this?" Mama inhaled and he heard her sob.

Anger started to swell in him. "I am gay and I'm not doing this to make you look bad or to get back at you for something you did. I can't change this, Mama. It is who I am and if you can't accept that I've fallen in love with a man then there's nothing for us to do except say goodbye."

"I can't accept that. It's against God, and what would the people in our neighborhood say if you were to date a man?" She paused for a second then continued, "You simply need to meet a good girl and she'll show you the error of your ways. You need a nice woman to cook and clean the house for you. Several of my friends have daughters who would be perfect for you."

"No!" He took a deep breath after he shouted at her. When he thought he had a handle on his anger, he said, "The love of a good woman isn't going to change me. I was born gay. I can't cover it up. Wait. I *won't* cover up the truth. I shouldn't have to because I should get the same respect Bogdan does from you."

He heard the click as she hung up on him. Resisting the urge to throw his phone across the room, he placed it gently on the end table before he buried his face in his hands. Hurt filled him and he didn't fight the tears from falling. Why couldn't his parents just be open minded enough to see that Ion wasn't going to change? All he wanted was for them to love him and Adrien like they did his brother and sister-in-law, but it certainly looked like that wasn't going to happen.

A buzzing drew his attention, and he looked at his phone to see Bogdan's number on the screen. He wasn't up to dealing with his brother, who he figured his mother had called to complain about Ion to. He wasn't going to get any support from Bogdan either. There wasn't any point in answering.

He let the call go to voicemail while he went to take a shower. After cleaning up, he changed into sweats and a T-shirt. Ion checked his phone before heading to his kitchen to make something to eat. He had two voicemails from Bogdan and he deleted them without listening to them.

An urge to talk to Adrien came over him, but he wasn't sure if he was done talking to Alain. So he decided to send him a text.

Alain show?

Ion got out his homework while his frozen dinner heated in the microwave. Once it was cooked, he sat at his table to eat and study. A few minutes later, his phone buzzed. Adrien had answered.

Yes. Still talking. Everything okay?

He smiled at the joy sweeping through him. Even though Adrien was busy, he still cared enough to ask how he was doing.

Not really, but we can talk tomorrow.

What happened?

As much as he wanted to talk to his lover, he knew Adrien was busy with Alain and he didn't want to distract him.

It's not important right now. Deal with your brother. Going to study for a little while then head to bed.

I'll be over when I get done here. It might be late, but I want to sleep with you tonight. Love you.

He discovered that he wanted to share his bed with Adrien and sleep in his arms.

All right. Tell your brother hello. Love you too.

Ion tossed his phone onto the table next to his books before getting back to reading and taking notes. After an hour or so, he put everything away and cleaned up before he settled on his couch. He would nap until Adrien got there.

* * * *

A knocking woke Ion and he rolled off the couch to stumble to his door. He checked through the peephole to make sure it was Adrien then opened it to let him in. After setting his bags down, Adrien embraced him tight.

"Sorry to wake you. I haven't put your key on my ring yet and forgot it at my place."

"It's all right." Ion kissed his cheek before stepping away. "Let's go to bed, love. It's been a long day for both of us."

Adrien didn't say anything until they were under the blankets, legs and arms entwined. Ion encouraged Adrien to lay his head on his chest. It was strange that they had only known each other for a few weeks, but already Ion hated sleeping without Adrien in his bed.

"How did your meeting go with Alain?" He ran his hand up and down Adrien's back.

"Fine. We reached an arrangement. I'm cutting his allowance in half, but he's not going to take a job at the office." Adrien didn't seem like he wanted to discuss his brother. "What happened to you?"

"Mama called and asked why I didn't come to dinner on Sunday." Ion closed his eyes as his anger and hurt rose inside him again.

Drawing him closer, Adrien asked. "What did you tell her?"

"Basically that I didn't come because I knew that you wouldn't be welcome there." He sniffed, not wanting to cry again.

"Oh, honey, you shouldn't cut yourself off from your family because of me," Adrien murmured.

"She asked why I was doing this to them. That I should stop being childish and trying to get back at them for something they didn't know they did. Like being gay is my way of punishing them for some slight." He tried to break away from Adrien's embrace, but his lover wouldn't let him. "She told me that several of her friends had daughters and she wanted me to meet them because it would just take the love of a good woman and I'd stop being gay."

"Well, she can introduce you with all the women she wants, I'm not letting go of you."

"I told her she should respect my decisions on who I love like she did Bogdan's, and she hung up on me." A tear dribbled down from the corner of his eye to disappear in his hair.

"I love you and my family adores you. You have Patrick and his sister, who I must say I'm looking forward to meeting. You're not alone even if they chose to turn their backs on you." Adrien brushed a kiss over his eyelids. "Maybe they'll change their minds after a while."

"Maybe, but I'm not waiting around for them to do so. I'm not letting go of you either, Adrien. I guess we're stuck with each other, huh?" Ion chuckled, a little sad that he was losing the family he'd always thought would be there for him.

"We are, but that's all right. There isn't anyone I'd rather be stuck with." Adrien yawned. "Let's try to get some sleep now. It's been an emotional night for both of us. We can talk more tomorrow."

Ion agreed and they snuggled together. He closed his eyes again, letting everything drift away from him.

* * * *

Oh wow. A warm, wet mouth wrapped around Ion's cock and he arched his back, trying to shove more of it in. When he heard someone gag, he opened his eyes then looked down to see Adrien lying between his legs with his lips stretched around Ion's shaft.

"Oh sorry. I thought it was a dream." He eased off a little and Adrien hummed.

Shuddering as the vibration ran along his length, Ion threaded his fingers in Adrien's hair before he slowly thrust in. Adrien took him like a pro and when Ion hit the back of his throat, Adrien swallowed.

"Fuck," he swore as he slipped out then pushed in.

Adrien didn't try to stop him or pull away. He took all that Ion gave him, allowing Ion to fuck his face as fast or slow as he wanted. Ion's head fell back and his eyes closed as his climax built in his groin.

"Adrien, love, I'm going to come," he warned, but Adrien didn't move. Electricity shot through Ion as he spilled his cum and Adrien swallowed it all. Ion trembled and cried out then he let his arms drop to the sheets beneath him.

He sighed as Adrien licked him clean then he grabbed Adrien's hand to get his lover to come up and kiss him. Ion tasted himself on Adrien's tongue and lips, but he tasted the unique flavor of Adrien as well.

As Ion reached for Adrien's cock, he asked, "How do you want me?"

Adrien shook his head. "I came when you did."

"Really?" Ion grinned. "That's cool."

"We need to get up. I thought I'd wake you instead of letting the alarm clock do it." Adrien pressed a quick peck on his cheek before rolling out of bed. "We should drop your sheets off at the cleaners, or do you have a washer and dryer in here?"

"I usually use the machines in the laundry room in the basement," Ion muttered as he joined Adrien in stripping the bed.

"No reason to do so today. Get some laundry together and we'll drop it off at my cleaners on the way to work," Adrien ordered.

As he walked to the bathroom, Ion stood there and stared after him. There was the CEO of a Fortune 100 company shining through, but while Ion might work for him, he didn't have to take orders from him when they weren't at the office.

"How about couching that as a request and not quite so demanding?" He kept his tone light, not wanting to tick Adrien off because it wasn't like he wouldn't take the man up on the offer of using his cleaners. He just didn't want it to sound like Adrien was telling him what to do.

Adrien looked at him from around the doorframe of the bathroom and grinned. "Sorry about that. Would you like to do that or we can just do them later when we get home?"

Ion shook his head. "Sorry. For some reason, I just got my back up hearing you say it that way. I know you're not ordering me around. You're spoiled and used to people doing whatever you want."

Holding out his hand, Adrien winked. "Yes, I am spoiled. That's what happens when you're rich and powerful. Will you come take a shower with me? I know your shower isn't big, but we can make it work."

There wasn't any way he'd say no to that offer. He took Adrien's hand, letting him draw him close.

"Does Mr Richardson know about us?" he asked as he watched Adrien turn the water on.

Adrien pursed his lips. "I'm not sure. I haven't said anything to him yet. Maybe I should mention it this morning during our meeting. That way if he finds out from someone else, he doesn't get mad because I didn't tell him personally."

"Who would he find out from? Patrick won't say a word to anyone." Ion stepped under the cascade of warm liquid.

"My family. Any one of them might say something to him. He didn't make it to my mother's party, so he'll call her to apologize and wish her a happy birthday. She might say how much she loved meeting you." Adrien joined him.

Ion nodded. "Is he going to be unhappy about you dating someone who works for you?"

"Sidney? Hell no." Adrien laughed. "I've dated an employee before. It's never changed how I treated him while at work. I haven't changed since we started dating, have I?"

"I don't think so, but of course, I worked in the mail room. It's not like I dealt with you on a daily basis or anything." He washed his hair then rinsed before switching places with Adrien.

"True. If he gives you any trouble, just let me know and I'll talk to him. He's usually pretty good about staying out of my business, but he is my best friend, so sometimes he just can't help himself." Adrien shot him a glance. "Kind of like Patrick and you."

Ion chuckled. "Something tells me when you and Mr Richardson go out, you hit some higher end clubs than Patrick and I."

"Oh hey, you want to go out dancing this weekend? Patrick can go with us and I'll see if Sidney is doing anything."

"Your straight friend will go to a gay club with us?" Ion stepped out of the tub to grab a towel.

Adrien burst out laughing. "Sidney isn't straight. He's bi, though he tends to go out in public with women. He saves his male lovers for private weekend getaways. I don't think he's completely ready to admit publicly that he likes guys."

"Oh."

Well...if Ion chose to tell Patrick about Sidney, his friend might decide to give it a chance, but Ion didn't think a man who hid his male partners was the man for Patrick.

"Do you think he'll ever come out totally?"

"Maybe for the right guy. I have the feeling he's not going to find the right woman." Adrien shrugged. "Considering how many he's dated and how many he's actually slept with, I think he's more gay than bi."

Grunting, Ion got dressed then grabbed some of his clothes to drop off at the cleaners. Adrien called Daniel to pick them up and they left Ion's apartment with time to spare.

Chapter Five

When they arrived at the office, Adrien kissed Ion before they climbed out of the car. He managed to keep his hands off Ion's ass while they rode the elevator. He didn't say a word when Ion got off on the twentieth floor where the troubleshooters department was.

Walking into his office, he spotted Patrick at his desk. "Glad to see you looking bright and cheerful this morning," he commented as he strolled past.

Patrick snorted. "It's a sunny day in the city and I happen to enjoy my job, sir."

Adrien snorted before asking, "Is Mr Richardson in yet?"

He set his briefcase on his desk before taking off his suit coat. He hung it up then accepted the cup of coffee Patrick held out for him.

"Yes, sir. I'll let him know that you're in."

"Thanks."

After sitting, he booted up his computer then pulled out the files he'd worked on yesterday at home while waiting for Alain to show up. Besides telling Sidney about dating Ion, he needed to talk to him about the financial issues the head of their London office had found.

His phone buzzed and when he hit the intercom, Patrick said, "Mr Richardson is here, sir."

"Send him in."

Sidney strolled in, carrying his own mug. "Good morning."

"It certainly is." He grinned, thinking about how he'd woken Ion that morning.

"I stopped by your place last night and you weren't there, but Alain was. He said you went to spend the night with your boyfriend." After sitting, Sidney eyed him. "I didn't know you were seeing anyone seriously."

"That's one of the things I wanted to talk to you about." Adrien frowned. "How did Alain look?"

Sidney shrugged. "Tired. Like he'd stayed up late too many nights in a row. Has he been hitting the gaming tables a little too hard lately?"

Adrien nodded. "Yeah. I told him I was cutting his allowance in half, and while he wasn't happy about it, he didn't complain either. I guess he figured there were worse things I could do, like take it all away from him."

Sipping his coffee, Sidney studied him. "So who is this mysterious boyfriend? Alain said you took him to meet your parents this weekend. He must be different—you've never taken one of your lovers home before."

"He is. I told him I'd talk to you about that this morning. I'm seeing Ion Vasile, the new guy in Bart's department." He relaxed back in his chair seeing the surprise appear on Sidney's face.

"Wait a minute. How long have you been seeing him?" Sidney looked suspicious.

"Our first date was after I offered him the promotion. Let him know that the position wasn't contingent on saying yes to me." Adrien rubbed his chin. "I took him to meet my parents because I love him, Sidney, and I want him in my life for a very long time."

Sidney blinked. "Wow. Isn't it rather quick to know you love Ion? You haven't been dating him that long. How many dates have you been on?"

Adrien took a sip before he said, "One."

"One? Just one? Shouldn't you go on a few more before you decide you love him?"

"Now you're the expert on dating? You date a bunch of women, but never sleep with any of them. You tell me you're bi, but you only have sex with men. I'm sorry to tell you, Sidney, but that makes you gay not bi."

Sidney stayed silent for a few minutes, and Adrien had a twinge of guilt. Yet he knew what he'd said was the truth. It was time for his friend to admit it and not try bullshit himself or anyone else.

Sighing, Sidney set his mug down then folded his hands over his stomach. "You're right about me, but I still think you need to date the man a few months before you tell him you love him."

"Too late. We've both said the 'L' word, and I want Ion to move in with me, but even I'll admit it's too soon for that." He pushed to his feet before pacing the length of his office. "The other thing is, my family loved him. Mother couldn't stop talking to him and Father thinks he has a lot of potential. Amelia and Jonathon both were impressed with Ion as well."

"You're joking, right?" Sidney grunted when Adrien shook his head. "I never thought your parents would accept any man you brought home. Not even if he was as rich as you, or one of the blue bloods here in the city."

"I thought the same thing, and I was worried that they would say something because Ion's from a blue collar family—no money and barely scraping by. That's one of the reasons why he came up with the proposal to save the Huntsman Toy Company. They all work there."

"Makes sense that he'd do whatever he could to help them out. Who else knows about you?"

Adrien gestured toward his outer office. "Patrick does because he's Ion's best friend, but other than that, only you here at work."

Sidney nodded. "Probably a good thing for a little while longer. Let him get settled in his new job and do some work for Bart before you let everyone else know."

"Thanks for the support. Now let's get down to business. Did you get the files from Winston?" They needed to discuss work, not Adrien's love life. It didn't matter what anyone else thought or said. He loved Ion and he was going to do everything he had to do to keep the man in his life.

Sitting up straight, Sidney lifted the tablet he'd carried with him before pulling up the files on his screen. Adrien went back behind his desk to sit, so they could do what they got paid for.

* * * *

Later that day, Adrien listened to the president of one of the companies he was selling. The man was trying to convince him not to sell the business, but Adrien saw no reason why he should keep it under the umbrella of Bellamy International. The company was doing well and could survive without any more help, so it was time to get rid of it.

While the man talked, Adrien slowly began to go back over what Sidney had said that morning. It was true. He needed to take Ion out on more dates, if only to prove he wasn't ashamed of being seen with the man.

He'd forgotten to ask Sidney if he wanted to go dancing with them that weekend. He'd text him when he was done with his lunch meeting.

"Are you listening to me, Bellamy?" the man enquired.

Adrien looked at him and shook his head. "No, I'm not."

He blinked at Adrien's honesty. "Why not? Is what I'm saying not important enough?"

"No." He held up his hand to keep him from saying anything. "I've told you several times that Bellamy has no reason to keep your company anymore. Selling it is a smart move for us and that's why I'm putting it on the block. If I didn't do it, then we'd eventually dismantle it and sell off the divisions. You wouldn't have a company to rule over any more."

Waving the waiter over, Adrien handed him his card. "I'll pay for this, but any more protests you might have won't be heard. Any emails you send me about this will be deleted. I'm done discussing this with you or anyone else. The next time I hear your company's name, it'll be on the sales papers."

"What about my job?"

He shrugged. "It'll be up to the new owners whether you keep it or not. I know you don't have the money to buy it yourself."

"Damn it. You're a cold-hearted son of a bitch, Bellamy." The man glared at him.

"It's just business." He signed the bill then took his card.

While he shrugged on his coat, he watched the man stalk out of the restaurant. Once he was by himself, he text Ion.

Do you have class tonight?

And he sent a text to Sidney about dancing that weekend. He stopped by the maître d' and got a reservation for that night. It was time he started courting Ion, even though he already knew how the man felt about him. His phone vibrated and he checked it.

No. Why?

I'm taking you out to dinner. I'll pick you up at seven. Dress nice.

All right. Love you.

Love you too.

Adrien headed out to where Daniel had the car waiting by the curb. "Back to the office, Daniel," he said as he climbed in.

"Yes, sir."

Sidney, who was flying out to Washington for business, text to let him know he'd meet them at Club

Wander at eleven on Saturday night. Adrien sent an okay back then tucked his phone in his pocket.

Leaning against the seat, he watched the skyscrapers of Manhattan slide past his window as Daniel made their way through traffic. Alain would be gone when he got back to his place that night. His brother had told him he would stop by their parents' to visit for the night then he was off to Hong Kong for some parties.

Adrien didn't like the thought of his brother mingling with the type of people that would be at those parties, but Alain was an adult and he swore to Adrien he wasn't in any danger. Well, Adrien didn't know about that and he knew he'd worry until Alain surfaced somewhere else.

He was glad that his brother was taking the time to see their parents though. Alyssa loved her youngest son, and it had hurt her when he hadn't shown up for her party. Adrien might not always see eye to eye with his family, but he loved his mother and didn't like it when she was unhappy.

His phone rang and he yanked it out to check the screen. *Speak of the devil.* "Hello, Mother."

"Adrien, thank you." The happiness in her voice flowed over the phone.

"I didn't do anything." Though he knew what she was talking about. "Is Alain still there?"

"He's out in the garage talking cars with your father."

"He seems to have picked up some knowledge from all those Formula One races he goes to around the world."

The car stopped and he waited for Daniel to get out and open the door for him. Adrien had learned that Daniel expected him to let him do his job, which meant opening a car door. When that happened, he climbed out before heading back into the building.

"At least he's learned one thing that will make his father happy. Did you talk to him about taking a job at the company?"

"Yes, Mother, but we decided it wasn't a good idea for him. I did cut his allowance in half and he knows that if he continues to overspend, I will cut him off." He hit the call button for the elevator. "I'm about to get on the elevator so I might cut out."

"I'll let you go. I know you're busy, but I just wanted to say thank you for reminding Alain to come visit."

"You're welcome. I'll call you on Sunday. Tell Father I love him."

She laughed. "I will, and please tell Ion we asked about him. I hope you two visit again soon."

"I'm sure we will. There's still a few more weeks of summer left and I'd like to take the boat out a couple more times."

"Wonderful. I'll talk to you on Sunday, Adrien. Love you." She hung up just as the elevator doors opened.

He walked on, nodding to some of the people in the car. After hitting the button for his floor, he leaned against the wall and thought about taking Ion to dinner that night. *Should I buy him flowers or something? I know most guys would think that was girly, but I want to get him something.*

Adrien got out on his floor and wandered toward his office. He was so caught up in his thoughts, he didn't notice the people gathered around Patrick's desk until he almost ran into one of them. Stopping, he folded his arms over his chest and waited to see how long it took to be noticed.

"Oh, my God, Patrick, I want one of those. It's gorgeous." One of the ladies lifted a necklace up in the air.

"I'll see what kind of deal I can get Patrice to make for you," Patrick said.

"Don't touch those."

Adrien's cock perked up at the sound of Ion's voice and he shifted on his feet, wishing he could adjust himself, but not wanting to draw attention to his crotch or himself. He did ease closer to see what Ion didn't want the women to touch.

It was a set of cuff links, and since he wasn't close enough, he couldn't really tell what they looked like. He glanced at his watch then walked back out of sight. Coughing to warn them, he approached again.

"Patrick," he said then stopped when he saw all the women were gone and only Ion stood there.

They had scattered like fish when a rock was thrown into the water. Adrien grinned as he walked up to Ion then brushed a kiss over his cheek.

"Did you have a good lunch?"

Ion kept one of his hands behind his back. "Yeah. Patrick and I met his sister."

"Great." He turned to look at Patrick. "I'm not accepting any calls from Henry Masters and any emails he might send can be deleted."

"Yes, sir." Patrick marked it down on a Post-it then stuck it on his computer screen. "Mr Tennant from the London office called. He'd like you to call him back as soon as you can."

"Thanks. Can you get him on the phone for me?" Adrien looked back at Ion. "Do you need Daniel to drive you home tonight?"

"No. I can take the subway. We still going out tonight?"

Adrien frowned as he saw that Patrick hadn't picked up the phone yet. "Yes. And Patrick, has Ion talked to you about going dancing on Saturday night? Sidney's going to meet us at Club Wander at eleven. We could grab something to eat before that."

Patrick blinked. "Yes, sir. I'm game to go. We've never been to Wander."

"That's because we can't afford it," Ion pointed out.

"Well, I've got us covered. Now we'd all better get back to work." Adrien touched Ion's cheek then went to his office.

Ion shot a glance over his shoulder to make sure Adrien had closed the door before he relaxed. "You don't think he saw these, do you?"

He held out the box with the cuff links in it. Patrick shook his head.

"I doubt it. Why are you getting them for him? It's not his birthday and you haven't been together long enough to start getting each other anniversary presents." Patrick picked up the phone after he looked up the London office's number.

Ion sighed. "He bought me a pair for his mother's party this weekend. I wanted to get him something."

"Okay. We need to get back to work. Call me tonight after you get done with dinner." Patrick held up his hand. "Never mind. I'll see you tomorrow and you can tell me what dinner was like."

Ion waved a hand in his friend's direction as he went back to his cubicle on the twentieth floor. He hid the jewelry box in his messenger bag then went back to work on a problem Bart had assigned him. It was something a few other people had tried to fix, but hadn't been able to. He figured it just needed a new set of eyes that didn't know the history behind the issue.

He got buried in the numbers and lost track of the rest of the day. It wasn't until Patrick poked him in the shoulder that he emerged from the fog. Ion glanced up to see his friend standing there smiling.

"Are you ready to go? I thought we could ride the subway together." Patrick stepped back.

"Sounds good to me." Patrick slid his file into his desk and locked it then grabbed his bag. "Let's go. I need to get home and clean up."

"Where are you going to dinner?"

They got an elevator and Ion didn't say anything because there were others riding down with them. He didn't want anyone to get curious and start asking questions.

Patrick seemed willing to wait until they were walking to the subway station. "So did he tell you where you were going?"

Ion frowned. "No. He just said to dress nice. I'm assuming that means a suit."

"More than likely. I wonder if he's taking you to Gramercy Tavern. That's where he had lunch. Maybe he decided to take you out on a date." Patrick bumped their hips together. "That's awesome."

"I'm not sure about that. I kind of like hanging out at our places together. Not having to worry whether people are thinking I'm not good enough for him."

They dashed down the stairs to the subway turnstiles. He swiped his MetroCard then stuffed it and his hands in his pockets as they stood on the platform.

"I get why you'd be worried, but seriously do you think Adrien believes that? He doesn't listen to what anyone else has to say." Patrick patted Ion's shoulder.

"Plus you said his family loved you. If you got the approval of Mr and Mrs Bellamy, you're golden."

"Do you think Adrien cares that much about what his parents think?" Ion snorted. "Hell, the way he talked about them, I thought for sure his mother would take one look at me and throw me as an imposter. She wasn't anything like that. None of them were like he told me they would be."

"Maybe he was just trying to give you the worst-case scenario," Patrick suggested as they pushed their way onto the subway car and found seats.

"He didn't need to worry me any more than I already was," Ion muttered. "I did like his parents, especially Alyssa. She was extremely nice."

Patrick snorted. "Really? I have to say I've never seen her smile or talk to any of us, except for Adrien and Mr Richardson. I just assumed that since I was just a personal assistant I wasn't important."

Shrugging, Ion grinned. "Maybe you weren't, or maybe she just hadn't been introduced to you and she takes those social things seriously. I don't know."

"Mr Richardson is going dancing with us?"

Ion had wondered how long it would be before Patrick asked him about that. He nodded. "Apparently Mr Richardson is bi or gay. Adrien wasn't completely clear on that, but he did say that most of Sidney's lovers have been men."

"So I have a chance?" Patrick's blue eyes sparkled.

"I would suggest you don't go after him, Patrick. He might be into men, but he isn't into coming out. Why do you think he dates all those women? He's not interested in being seen with a guy, just fucking them."

"I wouldn't mind that." Patrick wiggled his eyebrows and leered at Ion.

Ion laughed, but shook his head. "No. You deserve better than being Sidney's secret lover. You should be worshiped and spoiled by the man you love. Not shoved in the dark because he's not comfortable with himself."

Patrick threw his arm around Ion's shoulder then hugged him. "That's why you're my best friend. You always look out for me and you're right. As hot as I think Mr Richardson is, I don't want to be fucked in the dark while being ignored during the day."

"We both deserve that. You'll find your guy soon. I believe that, and while you're waiting, we'll go dancing and have some fun this weekend." Ion rested his head on Patrick's shoulder for a second before straightening.

Patrick let his arm drop as he winked. "Sounds good to me. I haven't gone to the clubs in a few weeks. Plus we're going to Wander, one of the hottest gay clubs in the city. I can't wait."

They started planning what they would wear and where they should go eat beforehand. It helped past the time while they rode and kept Ion from getting nervous about his dinner with Adrien that night.

Chapter Six

Adrien knocked on Ion's door and decided he was going to ask for a spare key that night. He'd already given Ion his spare one, so it was only fair that he got a key as well. Smiling, he held out the bouquet of flowers to Ion when the man opened his door.

"Oh wow. These are gorgeous." Ion took the dozen pink and white carnations then buried his face in them. "It's been a while since a guy got me flowers."

After stepping inside and closing the door behind him, Adrien said, "I wasn't sure about getting them because I was afraid you might think they were too girly. But then I said to hell with it. I like flowers and wanted to give them to you."

"I'm glad to know how you feel. I'll remember that." Ion strolled over to his kitchen area. "Let me put them in water then we can leave."

"Hey, do you have a spare key?" No time like the present to ask.

"Sure. It's in the top drawer next to the stove." Ion gestured in the direction of the oven.

Adrien got it out before he put it on his key ring. "You don't mind me having one?"

"No. Why would I? I meant to give it to you this morning before we left, but I forgot. It makes sense. I have a key to your place and you need one to mine so we don't have to wait until the other is home before we come over." Ion filled a vase, stuck the flowers in them then turned to throw his arms around Adrien.

Ignoring the fact that their suits were getting wrinkled, Adrien drew Ion close to kiss him. He crushed their lips together then swept his tongue in to taste the mint of Ion's toothpaste. Adrien let his hands slide down to grab two handfuls of Ion's ass and he wedged his thigh between Ion's legs.

He rocked his groin into Ion's and swallowed the moan escaping from Ion's throat. Adrien got lost in the flavor of Ion's mouth, letting the feel of their bodies moving against each other build his need. Yet he didn't want to come right then. He wanted to keep the tension high while they enjoyed a wonderful dinner and talked.

Easing away from Ion, he took a deep breath while trying to gain control of his lust. Ion pouted when he realized Adrien wasn't going to take it any further.

"We're going to be late if we do anything right now. I don't want to miss our reservations," Adrien said, dropping his hands from Ion's butt.

"Come on. We can go out to eat later. I want you," Ion pleaded, reaching out to press his palm against the bulge in Adrien's pants.

Adrien groaned as he arched into Ion's touch, but he gripped Ion's wrist before removing him from his groin. "As much as I'd like to do just that, I also want to take you out on a date. We've only been on one and I thought it would be fun for us."

Ion sighed, still looking a little disappointed and Adrien chuckled.

"Trust me. I'll be fucking you when we get back here," he promised.

"You'd better." Ion glared as he snatched up his keys, wallet and phone before they left.

Daniel held the car door open and Ion climbed in before Adrien. His driver knew where they were going, so Adrien simply embraced Ion as they settled back in the seat. He nuzzled Ion's temple.

"Did you have a good rest of the day?"

Ion shrugged. "It was interesting. I'm enjoying the job."

"Great. I spent the afternoon talking to Winston Tennant about those finances he'd sent me." Adrien grimaced when he thought about the mess those were in. "I'm not sure how it slipped through our vetting process when we looked at purchasing the company."

"Is that Mr Tennant's fault?" Ion had his eyes closed while he rested against Adrien.

"To be honest, it's all of our faults. Winston might be the head of the London office, but ultimately any decision to buy is up to me. I don't remember seeing anything like that in any of the files I read." He pursed his lips as he thought then said, "Of course, all of the problems could have happened during the switch over. Winston's coming over in a week or two and we're going over everything together. Sidney will be joining us as well."

Ion hummed softly so Adrien knew he was listening.

"You know, we should introduce Patrick to Winston. I think they'd be a good match."

He smirked as Ion pushed far enough away to look him in the eye. "What are you talking about? Are you going to try your hand at matchmaking?"

"Possibly. I've been friends with Winston for several years now, ever since he first started working for my father. We kind of rose through the ranks together and his father is an old friend of my father's from Oxford."

Adrien took a moment to remember those summers he'd spent in England with Winston and Sidney, rowing on the Thames or boating along the coast. It had been perfect but then it had become time for all of them to take their places in the family businesses and Winston had lost his sense of fun.

"He got married because it was what his father expected of him, but in the only act of rebellion I've ever seen him do, he divorced her and came out. His father wasn't pleased and that's why Winston's working for me now instead."

"And you think he'd be a good match for Patrick? You do realize that Patrick isn't the type to hide his light under a basket right? There's no way anyone meeting him and talking to him for the first time won't know that he's gay." Ion took Adrien's hand in his.

Adrien brought Ion's knuckles up to his mouth so he could place a kiss on them. "I know that and it'll be great to watch Winston deal with that. He's not in the closest, but he's very restrained about everything, not just his sex life. I don't think the man's been laid in a few years, in fact. His father disowning him kind of took the life out of him. Do you know what I mean?"

"Yeah. I totally understand what you mean." Ion played with Adrien's fingers while he thought. "Maybe you're right. It can't hurt, anyway. We can have Patrick show Winston around the city while he's here and we'll go out dancing again."

"Once you meet Winston, you'll see why I think Patrick is perfect for him. Now if I can just get

Sidney's head out of his ass and find him someone, I'll be happy."

"You've turned into one of those people." Ion stared at him in horror.

He frowned. "One of those people? What do you mean?"

"You're now in a serious relationship and you're happy, so you want all of your friends to be happy as well. I think you're going to find it harder than you imagine to hook them up with good men." Ion exhaled loudly. "Has your brother left yet?"

"Now you're trying to change the subject, but I'll let you because I don't think it's going to be that hard. I know my friends and I can pick out the right men for them."

Ion glared at him. "What if Sidney doesn't want a man? What if he'd be perfectly happy with a woman?"

Adrien shook his head. "No. If he wanted a woman, he could've settled down with any of the hundreds he's dated over the years. Not one of those relationships lasted more than a month each. Most of those ladies were wonderful girls. They weren't after him for his money or his place in society. They sincerely liked him, but he wasn't into them."

"I think you're going to get yourself into trouble with all this match making. Why not try setting your brother up with someone?"

"Alain doesn't have the time or the kind of lifestyle that's conducive to finding everlasting love. And to answer your question, he's spending the night with my parents then leaving for Hong Kong tomorrow. There's some kind of big gaming event there that he doesn't want to miss." Adrien glanced around when the car slowed then stopped. "We're here."

Ion studied him for a moment. "We're going to talk about all of this later. Right now, I'm going to enjoy the fact that I'm on a date with one of the most eligible men in New York. Everyone's going to be so jealous of me."

"I think they're going to be too busy lusting after you, they won't even notice me." Adrien winked before he stepped from the car.

"You're full of shit, but flattery will get you laid, love," Ion murmured as he joined him on the curb.

He strolled into Gramercy Tavern arm in arm with Ion and smiled at the maître d' as the man greeted them. They were shown to a private table closer to the back of the restaurant, which was fine with Adrien. He wasn't there to be seen by all the important people. He was there to enjoy a nice dinner with the man he loved.

After holding out Ion's chair for him, Adrien pushed it in when Ion sat then went to take his own seat next to him. He didn't want to sit across from him. This way he could touch Ion as much as he wished. The waitress came over and Adrien ordered a bottle of their best red and an appetizer.

"What's good here?" Ion started to open the menu, but Adrien stopped him.

"I think we'll get the seasonal tasting. It gives us a little taste of a lot of different things. I always enjoy that instead of getting the same old thing every time."

Ion grinned at him. "I'll let you take charge tonight, but one night you and I are going out and I'll treat you to one of my favorite places to eat."

"Sounds good to me." He took Ion's hand in his again. "Have you heard from your mother again?"

"No, and I don't think I will. She doesn't apologize to us. We're the ones who are supposed to grovel and say we're sorry to her. Even when we aren't the ones who are wrong."

Adrien sniffed. "My mother is much like that, though I think it's only with Amelia and I that she acts that way. She's very forgiving with Alain. Yet I think she's finally coming to the end of her rope with him."

"Missing her birthday party when he knows how big a deal it is to her probably rubs her the wrong way," Ion commented. "I wouldn't be surprise if she makes him grovel quite a bit because of that."

Adrien wasn't convinced of that, but he wasn't interested in discussing his brother any more. He looked at Ion. "Where did your parents emigrate from?"

Ion gave him a narrow-eyed look, but went with the conversation. "They came from a small town in Romania. It was difficult for them to get here because of the communists being in charge when they thought about coming, but they did it. Pops says he came because he wanted to give his children a better life than he had."

"And it worked." He stopped to give their entrée order to the waitress along with what they wanted to drink. Once she left, he went back to what they'd been talking about. "Was it difficult for them to adjust?"

"Mama said learning English was the hardest for her and she doesn't always get the words right. Or she'll just speak in Romanian. We spoke a lot of it in our house." Ion's fond expression told Adrien he liked those memories.

"That's marvelous," Adrien said. "I can speak Chinese and Japanese fluently, and make myself understood in a couple other languages, but it's not something that was easy for me to learn. I kind of wish I'd learned it at a much younger age than I did."

"But being fluent in some foreign languages is always good for the CEO of an international company."

The waitress returned to decant the wine and while she did so, Adrien placed his hand on Ion's thigh then slid it up to brush his pinkie against the zipper of Ion's pants. Ion jerked, but didn't look at him. Adrien tasted the wine before nodding and she poured out some for each of them. He turned his hand to press his palm to the growing bulge while taking another sip.

Once she left, Ion turned to glare at him. "What are you doing?"

"Just having a little fun," he murmured as he leaned closer to place his lips a few inches from Ion's ear. "I thought I'd keep the lust simmering, so we have something to look forward to when we get home."

"Just remember that simmering can turn to boiling. I might embarrass you by dropping to my knees and giving you a blow job under the table."

Just the thought of Ion on his knees in front of him made Adrien harder than he'd ever been. He inhaled sharply as he shifted in his chair. Ion's grin held a bit of evil in it.

"That wasn't very nice." Adrien pouted for a second, then he matched Ion's grin with one of his own. "Maybe I'll be the one to do it. I think I can fit under here."

Flexing his fingers, he felt Ion's erection twitch slightly in his hand. Before Ion could say anything to that comment, a throat being cleared got them both to look up. Adrien stood, offering his hand to the older man standing next to the table.

"Bill, nice to see you."

"And you as well, Adrien. How are your parents doing?" Bill shook Adrien's hand then tilted his head to Ion.

"They're doing well. Father has been caught up in his racing team and Mother still enjoys her charities." Adrien gestured toward Ion. "This is my boyfriend, Ion Vasile. Ion, this is Bill Pater, a dear friend of my parents."

Ion stood and Bill shook his hand as well. Adrien had never known Bill to care about Adrien's sexual preference. He'd always treated him the same.

"Wonderful to meet you, Ion. I'll let you two get back to your meal. I just wanted to say hello, and please let your parents know I asked after them."

"I will." He waited until Bill had walked away before he sat. Ion slowly sat and Adrien glanced at him and saw the rather stunned expression on Ion's face. "What?"

"He didn't even blink when you introduced us," Ion pointed out.

"Yes. So?" He acknowledged the waitress as she set their appetizer in front of them.

Ion took a bite of the Beef Tartare then chewed and swallowed before he replied. "I guess I never thought people in your circle of society would be as open minded as they seem."

"The thing is, I don't think Bill would be nearly as open minded if it was his son or daughter who was gay. He can be accepting because I'm not related to him. For some people, it's perfectly fine if someone else's child is different, but they don't want their own to be." Adrien shrugged. "I don't do business with Bill, so I don't have to give a fuck what he thinks about me."

"He isn't a friend of yours?"

"No. He and his wife play tennis with my parents from time to time, and since they've already met you and love you, we don't have to worry about what he says to them." Adrien hummed in appreciation at the taste of the tartare. "I do love this place."

Ion didn't say anything else and they finished the appetizer in silence. Then as the rest of their food slowly appeared over the course of two hours, Adrien got to know Ion better. They chatted about favorite movies and books. He drew his lover out, and the more he found out, the deeper in love he fell.

After dessert, he paid the bill and they went outside where Daniel had the car waiting for them. Adrien pulled Ion into his arms as soon as Daniel shut the door behind them. Taking Ion's lips, he tasted the bite of the wine and the hint of sweetness from sugar. He stroked his tongue along Ion's, encouraging his lover to play with him.

He made out with Ion the entire way back to Ion's apartment, and he ran his hands over Ion's hard body, touching the spots that he knew would turn Ion on. He wanted him so excited that he wouldn't wait to reach the bedroom before he begged Adrien to fuck him.

Adrien grinned as Ion dragged him from the car then into the building. He was a little disappointed that there was another couple in the elevator with them because he would've enjoyed continuing to stoke the flames of desire burning in Ion.

Once they were inside the apartment, Adrien grunted when Ion shoved him back against the door before dropping to his knees in front of him. He tensed in anticipation as Ion got his belt undone then his pants open.

Just at the moment Ion put his mouth around the head of Adrien's cock, a phone rang. Adrien groaned, knowing it wasn't his, but the way Ion jerked told him that his lover was going to answer it.

"I'm sorry," Ion said from where he crouched. "It's Olive's ring tone. She wouldn't be calling me unless it was something truly important."

"Go ahead." Adrien let his head drop back and thump against the wood of the door. He listened as Ion dug through his pockets to find his phone.

"Hello, Olive. What's wrong?"

Adrien opened his eyes then looked at Ion. The surprise and concern that crossed his face had Adrien tucking his dick back into his pants before refastening them. Reaching down, he grabbed Ion's arm to lift him to his feet.

"Are you sure? Which hospital? All right. We'll be there as soon as we can."

He hung up and Adrien asked, "Where are we going?"

"Mount Sinai Queens," Ion muttered.

"Let's go." Adrien wasn't about send Ion off to the hospital on his own, not that Ion had suggested it or anything. "Who's sick?"

"My brother."

Chapter Seven

Ion was numb as Adrien bundled him into a cab. He heard him tell the cabbie where they needed to go, but he couldn't get his mind to move past the fact that his brother was in critical condition after a car accident.

"Ion, what happened to Bogdan?" Adrien held his hand. His grip kept Ion in the present and stopped him from going into hysterics.

"Olive didn't say much, just that he was in ICU after an accident when he was driving home from work." Ion looked at Adrien. "He usually comes home around six. Why didn't anyone call me before this?"

Adrien shrugged. "They might have been crazy with having to get someone to take care of the kids and find out all the information they could before calling you."

Even in shock, Ion knew that was a weak excuse. "I wonder if maybe my parents just didn't consider calling me. Obviously Olive called as soon as she could, but you'd think Mama would've let me know as soon as she heard."

"Honey, don't borrow trouble. Wait until we get there and find out what's going on. If you worry about it now, you're just going to get more worked up than you need to be." Adrien encircled Ion's shoulders then pulled him close.

Closing his eyes, Ion breathed deeply and Adrien's familiar, expensive cologne filled his nostrils. Knowing Adrien was there to lean on helped take some of Ion's tension away. He entwined their fingers, gripping him tightly.

He might not have been happy with his family and had hoped his brother would've supported him more. None of that mattered right at the moment. All that he cared about was finding out how badly his brother was injured and what was being done to save him.

His phone rang again, but he couldn't answer it. Adrien took it from him and answered.

"Hello?" He paused. "This is Adrien, Ion's boyfriend. We're on our way. We were at Ion's apartment, so depending on how heavy traffic is, we should be there in thirty minutes."

Another pause. Ion felt Adrien's gaze on him, but he didn't look up.

"Yes, ma'am. I understand, but you do realize that Bogdan is his brother and he has the right to go see him."

Stiffening, Ion pulled away from Adrien to stare at him.

"Olive called him, Mrs Vasile, and it seems to me if she didn't want him there, she would've told him not to come."

His mother had called to tell him not to come to the hospital. *What a load of bullshit.* He didn't care what his parents wanted. He was going to see his brother and if Olive said she didn't want him there, then he'd leave.

"I'm sorry to hear that, ma'am. But we're still coming and if you chose not to talk to us, that is your problem. I would hope you could put your concerns aside and allow Ion to be at his brother's side during all of this."

Adrien met Ion's eyes and he could see the anger building in them as Adrien listened to whatever Ion's mother was telling him.

"Again, I'm sorry, ma'am. We'll be there in a little while then you and your husband can discuss your issues with Ion if you choose. It's not my place to tell him anything."

Ion watched Adrien hang up then hand the phone back to him.

"That was your mother. She's very unhappy that you're coming to push your presence and unnatural relationship on them during this trying time."

"Is that what she said?" It sounded rather too well-spoken to be what his mama had actually said.

"I might be paraphrasing slightly."

Ion dove back into Adrien's embrace. "If I wasn't so freaked out right now, I would say to hell with it and go back to home. But it's not like Bogdan got into a fender bender or anything. Olive sounded really worried and he's in ICU."

"Like I told your mother, we'll go to the hospital and talk to Olive. If your sister-in-law doesn't want us there, we'll leave. But if she does, we'll stay no matter what your parents have to say about it." Adrien tightened his hold on Ion. "Do you think she'll send you away?"

Lifting one shoulder in a half shrug, Ion said, "I don't know. I haven't talked to her since this whole thing started and she's never commented one way or the other when I came out."

"She lets you see the kids, doesn't she?" Adrien slipped his hand under Ion's jacket to stroke his hand up and down his back.

"She did. I've been so busy with you that I haven't thought about going to see them. Now with this whole thing blowing up, she might not let me. It would depend on what Bogdan says."

"Is he the ruler in that family?"

Ion snorted. "He likes to think so, but I've seen Olive tell him off. Their marriage certainly isn't like our parents. Mama would never dream of disagreeing with Pops. She's a dutiful wife."

Adrien nuzzled Ion's temple. "They're from a different generation, love. You have to keep that in mind."

He wasn't in the mood to make allowances for his parents, not caring about where they came from or what people their age thought. *Why should I let their actions go just because they're from a different generation? Being from a different time doesn't mean they can't change.*

The taxi slowed in front of the hospital and Ion barely waited for the vehicle to stop before he jumped out. He rushed in while Adrien paid the driver, then found himself standing in the lobby, trying to figure out where he needed to go.

After entering, Adrien took his elbow and escorted him to the reception desk. "My partner's brother was brought in earlier this evening. Could you tell us what floor ICU is on?"

"Yes, sir." She gave them the floor and directed them to the elevators.

Ion leaned on Adrien the entire ride up to ICU. Olive was standing right there when the doors slid open. She took one look at Ion and burst into tears. Holding out his arms, he wasn't sure what she'd do, but he wanted to comfort her. His heart jumped when she threw herself into his embrace.

Adrien ushered them out of the way, then stood between them and anyone else in the hallway. Breathing deep, Ion tried to get control of his emotions. He was scared to death about Bogdan, but to know Olive wasn't turning her back on him helped him gain a little control.

"Oh, honey, what happened?" He eased her away from him so he could see her face.

A handkerchief appeared over his shoulder and he took it before handing it to Olive. She let her gaze go to Adrien.

"Is this your boyfriend?"

Ion took a deep breath before introducing them. "Yes. Adrien Bellamy, this is my sister-in-law, Olive Vasile."

"It's nice to meet you, though I wish it was under better circumstances." Adrien's voice was gentle.

Olive blinked and Ion figured Adrien was smiling at her.

"His smile has the same effect on me," he told her as he winked.

Giggling, she wiped her eyes then sighed. "Bogdan was driving home and someone rear ended him. His car was smashed between the vehicle that hit him and the truck in front of him. They had to use the Jaws of Life to get him out and he just got out of surgery. He's in a medically induced coma because he has swelling in his brain and they want to let it go down before they bring him out of it. He's also on a ventilator."

As Ion swallowed hard, his hands began to shake. Adrien took one of them in his and Olive took the other.

"What do the doctors say? Do they think he'll be all right?"

"They are cautiously optimistic. Just like always. No point in getting our hopes up or anything."

Ion glanced at Adrien and his lover encircled his waist, letting him rest his weight on him. "How are his doctors? Does he have good ones?"

She shrugged. "I don't know. They might be."

Adrien gave Ion a hard hug then stepped away. "Why don't I make some calls? I know some surgeons and they might be able to tell me who we should have looking after Bogdan."

"Oh, we can't afford it. Our health insurance is going to barely cover this as it is," Olive protested.

Ion knew what Adrien was going to say, and though his pride argued that they shouldn't accept charity, his practical side shouted that Adrien had the money and was willing to help.

"I'll cover any costs that your insurance doesn't, Mrs Vasile. You don't need to worry about it at all. Just pray and be there for your husband." Adrien kissed Ion quickly. "I'm going down to the lobby where I can make some calls without bothering anyone. Text me if you need me. I'll be back up when I'm done."

He and Olive watched Adrien stride away toward the bank of elevators. Once he disappeared behind the doors, Olive looked at Ion.

"Is he serious?"

Nodding, Ion offered her his arm. "Yes. While our first inclination is to say no and be proud, we have to be realistic. We'll be paying off the bills for decades to come. I wish we could afford to say no, but to be honest, I believe that even if we said no, Adrien would go behind our backs and pay for it anyway."

Olive frowned then realization dawned in her eyes. "Are you telling me that your boyfriend is *that* Adrien Bellamy, head of Bellamy International? One of the richest men in the city and the new owner of Huntsman Toy Company?"

Ion chuckled. "Yes, that would him."

"Holy shit!" She kept her voice low as they approached Bogdan's room. "I had no idea."

"I didn't tell anyone who I was dating. You would've met him last Sunday if Mama hadn't acted like I was committing the worse sin in the entire world by bringing him." He frowned.

His sister-in-law stopped him. "Is that why Bogdan has been so upset this week? He wouldn't tell me, but I know your mother has been calling him all the time."

Ion sighed. Talking about it right then wasn't going to help anything and he wanted to see Bogdan himself. "Can we talk about this later?"

Olive nodded. "Of course. Go in and sit with him for a little bit. I'm going to call your mama to let her know what's happening. I sent them home once Bogdan got out of surgery. They don't need to be here all night, plus I needed someone to watch the kids."

He squeezed her hand before going into the room. All kinds of machines surrounded Bogdan and tears began to fill Ion's eyes. He'd been angry with him for seeming to take their parents' side, but he'd never thought he'd see his big brother laid low like this. He wanted to touch Bogdan, yet there didn't seem to be any place not covered with bruises or bandages.

The only reassurance Ion received was from the whoosh and whirl of the machines helping Bogdan breathe. He listened to the beep of the monitor as it sounded Bogdan's heartbeat. Ion stood at the end of his bed, staring at him, and tears rolled down his cheeks.

Adrien walked back in and said, "Come on, love. I need to talk to Olive then we should go home. You can come back tomorrow and spend all weekend here if you want. Plus you have emergency time you can take and if you need more, I'll talk to the HR department. We can work something out."

Adrien took his hand, leading him from the room. Ion glanced back once before he followed Adrien to where Olive stood by the nurse's station.

"I called some people I know. One of the best neurosurgeons in the country will be here tomorrow morning to talk with you and to look over Bogdan's charts. We went to Oxford together and he's doing this as a favor to me. If he thinks there is anything else he can do differently from what they're doing here, he'll let us know."

Olive threw her arms around Adrien, giving him a huge hug. "Thank you so much, Mr Bellamy."

"Please, call me Adrien. We're family now and since I don't ever plan on letting Ion get away from me, we're going to be in each other's lives for a very long time." Adrien kissed her cheek. "Are you staying tonight or are you heading home?"

"I was just waiting for Ion to get here. Now that you've come, I'm going to head to Mama's to pick up the children. I'll be back in the morning. They won't let us sit in the rooms for long while he's in ICU, but we can come in for short periods. Were you coming back in the morning as well, Ion?"

"I'll spend as much time as I can here this weekend. I'll have to talk to my boss at Bellamy and see what my options are for taking time off during the week."

"Do you want me to set up a schedule so you're not here when your parents are?" Olive asked. "I know it's going to be hard enough to see Bogdan like this. Dealing with your mama can be trying on the best of days."

They shared a laugh and Ion rubbed his chin. "No. Don't worry about keeping us apart. If she chooses to make a scene while we're here, that's on her. I'm not going to argue or debate with either of them about my life. I'm just glad you're still on my side."

"Why wouldn't I be? My best friend and her wife watch the kids all the time. I don't care who you love as long as you're happy." She hugged him again. "Now go home and take your wonderful boyfriend with you. I'll text you in the morning to let you know when I'm going to be here."

"I love you, Olive. If you need anything, you let me know." He embraced her back.

"No matter what, you tell us. We'll get it for you as soon as we can." Adrien took his turn getting a hug.

Ion held on to Adrien's hand as they left the hospital. He didn't say anything until they were almost back to his apartment.

"I should call Patrick and let him know. He cares about Bogdan like he's his big brother." He fumbled with his cell.

"Don't worry. I already took care of it and Patrick is meeting us at your place. He'll spend the night and go to the hospital with you. I have a meeting first thing in the morning that I can't miss, but Patrick will go to make sure the neurosurgeon gets there okay."

"I can take care of things myself you know," he pointed out, even though he didn't feel very together at the moment.

"Of course you can, and as this situation continues, you're going to have to be strong for Olive. Let me be strong for you right now. I'm a little more removed from the shock of it, so I can focus on the things that need to be done while you be there for your family." Adrien held out his hand. "More than likely, there will be a time when I'm going to need you to be strong for me. That's what being part of a serious couple means. We take turns being the rock when the other needs to lean."

Ion took Adrien's hand then brought it up to his mouth. He brushed a kiss over Adrien's knuckles. "I love you so much."

"And I love you."

* * * *

Patrick was waiting for them in Ion's apartment and he hugged Ion tight. "I'm so sorry. I couldn't believe it when Adrien called me. I let my parents and Patrice know. They'll stop by your parents' tomorrow to see if they need anything."

Nodding, Ion realized he was exhausted and all he wanted was to curl up in Adrien's arms and rest. Maybe when he woke the next morning, he'd find out it had all been a terrible dream.

"I think we should all head to bed, gentlemen. Tomorrow is the start of a very long road ahead of all of us," Adrien suggested.

Neither he nor Patrick complained, and within thirty minutes, Ion crawled under his blankets to join Adrien. Patrick slept out on the couch. Adrien pulled Ion tight against him before placing a kiss on his lips.

"Try to sleep, love. I'm here and you're not going to have to be strong on your own," Adrien informed him.

Ion murmured, "I love you too," but didn't think he was going to be able to get a wink. Yet the warmth of Adrien's embrace combined with the crash of his emotions dragged him into the darkness.

Chapter Eight

When he and Patrick stepped out onto the ICU floor the next morning, Ion spotted his mother exiting Bogdan's room. He tensed, but Patrick ignored him to walk over to her and give her a hug.

"Mama Vasile, I'm so sorry. I've always thought of Bogdan as an older brother. I'm here if you need me for anything," Patrick told her.

"You're a good boy, Patrick." She patted his cheek, but her gaze shot over to where Ion stood. "Olive told me you were coming this morning, so I stayed because I wish to talk to you."

"Yes, Mama." Ion didn't offer to hug her or kiss her cheek. She wasn't very welcoming anyway.

"Patrick, sit with Bogdan until Olive comes back. She had to go and drop the boys at their babysitter's."

"All right." Patrick slapped Ion on the shoulder before he went into the room.

"We'll go down to the cafeteria so we can talk."

He let her lead the way, knowing by the set of her shoulders that she wasn't happy with him. *No shit, Sherlock. Doesn't take a genius to know she doesn't want you around.* But he would stand his ground because Olive did want him there and until she said otherwise, he would be here for her.

They got some coffee then found an out-of-the-way table. She took a sip before looking at him.

"Olive told me what your friend is doing for us. I wish you to tell him thanks, but no. We can't take his money."

"I will tell him no such thing, Mama. Adrien is doing this out of the goodness of his heart. He has the money and he doesn't see the point of Olive and Bogdan going into debt because of his hospital bills when he can pay them." Ion held on his mug so tightly, he was afraid it was going to shatter in his hand.

His mama stared at him. "We don't need help from him. It is bad enough you think you are in love with him and that you are telling people he is your boyfriend. I won't be indebted to his kind."

"His kind? You make him sound like some strange alien creature. Is it because he's gay or because he's rich that you don't like him?" Ion's anger began to rise. "Let go of your pride and bigotry, Mama. Adrien is a good man who is only trying to help us. He doesn't want Bogdan or Olive to worry about anything except getting better."

"Your father is going to talk to Olive about accepting that man's help and I'm sure she'll see why we can't take charity." She'd chosen to ignore his question, but Ion knew that it was probably a little bit of both reasons making her act that way.

"I'm pretty sure that's not going to happen, but I have to warn you that if it does, Adrien's just going to sneak around behind your backs and pay the bills anyway. I know him and he'll do it because it'll make me feel better." Ion grinned. "Adrien loves me and will do anything to make my life easier."

She winced when he said 'love' and he wanted to shake her. He wanted to demand she tell him how their loving each other in some way affected her or Pops.

Her smile was strained, showing how difficult talking to him was for her. Ion didn't care if it made her uncomfortable. She needed to hear what he had to say and whether she accepted him and Adrien afterwards was up to her.

"How does Pops feel about this?"

To be honest, he wondered if his father even knew what the fuss was about. There had been times while he was growing up when his mother had hidden things from his dad because she hadn't thought they were important enough to bother him with. *Is having me want to introduce them to my male lover important enough for her to interrupt his ball game?*

"Your father feels the same as I do," she informed him, but she shifted her gaze away from him when she said it and Ion wasn't a hundred percent convinced.

His phone vibrated and he checked the screen to read Patrick's text. "Patrick says that both Olive and the neurosurgeon Adrien asked to check over Bogdan's case are here. Were you coming back upstairs with me or is being in my presence bothering you too much?"

"I'll go home. Olive can tell me what the doctor said later. Tell Patrick goodbye for me." His mama stood.

"Why don't you have a problem with Patrick being gay, but you act like it's a mortal insult because I am?" It was a question that had been annoying him for quite some time.

"Patrick is not my son. His actions do not reflect on me in the community, so it does not matter whether he is straight or gay. And if the Gaversons aren't upset by how their son acts, then it is none of my business. But you're my son and what you do is a direct reflection on how I raised you. I'm not a terrible mother. You shouldn't hate women like you do."

Shock caused his mouth to drop open. *What the fuck?*

"Who said I hated women? If I did, why would I do any of this for Olive? Why would I be good friends with Patrick's sister?" Ion growled under his breath. "I'm not gay because I hate you, Mama. I'm gay because that was the way I was born. It has nothing to do with you."

After standing, he reached out but stopped an inch from her arm. She'd stiffened like she was afraid he'd contaminate her with his touch. Ion took a deep breath and let his hand drop to his side.

"I'm going to be with Olive and Bogdan until he — or she — tells me to go away. We'll work out a schedule or something so that you and I will never have to run into each other again. I wouldn't want you to be infected by me. And God forbid I make you look bad in front of the neighbors. I'm sorry about that, but I'm not going to deny who I am and how much I love Adrien to make you happy."

He left her standing there to head back up to Bogdan's room. Olive and Patrick were waiting in the hallway when he arrived.

"Where's Mama?" Olive asked then held out a tissue. "Never mind. I guess she went home."

Wiping his cheeks, Ion said, "Yeah. She didn't want to be around me any more in case I touched her or something. Like you can catch the gay or something."

"Yet she hugged me without any problem," Patrick pointed out.

"I know, but you're not her son, Patrick. You embarrass your parents, not her, so she's fine with that." Ion wrinkled his nose. "Is someone with Bogdan?"

"The neurosurgeon Adrien asked to look Bogdan over is in there. He asked us to step outside while he went over his charts and checked him out." Olive motioned toward the room. "When he comes out, he'll tell us if there's anything that needs to be done or if he can do something different that will help him."

"How about we go down to the cafeteria and I'll have Goran meet us down there when he's done?" Patrick suggested.

"Sounds good to me. I never did get to finish my coffee."

Olive placed her hand in the crook of Ion's elbow. "She might be your mother, Ion, but until Bogdan tells me that he doesn't want you around, you're going to stay by my side. I need you to help me through this."

"Thanks, Olive. I appreciate it more than you can say." He gave her a quick kiss on the cheek then they headed toward the elevator. He felt his phone vibrate in his pocket. After getting it out, he smiled when he saw the name on the screen. "It's Adrien, but I'll call him back when we get downstairs."

Once they were sitting at a table near a bank of windows, Ion dialed Adrien's number.

"Hello, love. How are things going at the hospital?" Adrien asked when he answered.

"I guess it's going fine. Your friend is with Bogdan now and we'll talk to him when he's done. My mom was here." He stopped to take a breath.

Adrien hummed, apparently waiting for Ion to continue. He let his breath go and tried to relax. He would deal with his mother's rejection later. Right now, he had to see what the prognosis for his brother was.

"How did she handle seeing you?" Adrien pushed.

"She acted like I was contagious and told me I hated women."

Olive gasped while Adrien snorted in his ear.

"Seriously? She thinks you're gay because you hate women?"

Olive looked outraged.

Adrien chuckled. "She just doesn't get the whole gay is in your DNA, does she?"

"No and to be honest, I don't want to discuss it at the moment. I want to stay focused on Bogdan and what we can do to help him when he gets out of the hospital." He shoved any emotions he might have had deep down inside. At some point, it would boil over, but he didn't care. He'd deal with it when it happened.

"My mother and Amelia will be stopping by at some point today. They're in the city to do some shopping and attend some meetings. They wanted to say hello and to meet your sister-in-law," Adrien informed him. "I have meetings all day so I won't be able to come out there until after six."

"I'll text you, but I think I'll probably have gone home by then. With Bogdan still unconscious, there's no reason why I should stay too late." Ion met Olive's gaze and she agreed.

"Do that, honey. Just let me know which apartment you're at and I'll bring dinner home with me."

Ion heard a voice in the background of Adrien's call. "You should get back to your meetings. I'll text you later and I love you."

"I love you too, and so does the rest of my family. Remember that, Ion. You still have family. Olive, Bogdan and mine. They all love you and maybe someday your parents will come around."

"Maybe. Talk to you later." He ended the call then took a sip of his coffee. As much as he didn't want to think about his family, he had to ask. "Do you know what Pops has to say about any of this, Olive? Has he asked why I haven't been around or anything like that?"

"Actually I think he talked to Bogdan about it yesterday before the accident. At least, Bogdan said something about talking to his father at lunch about family things." Olive patted Ion's hand. "I don't know what they said to each other, but he did want to know."

"What did Bogdan say to you?" Ion flopped his hand back and forth.

Olive smiled. "He wasn't happy about how you were ignoring your mother, though I think that was mostly because she spent more time bothering him."

Ion fidgeted with his mug. "He asked me why I couldn't humor them. Why I needed to bring Adrien to dinner. He didn't sound happy about it."

"I know he's never seemed like he supported you, Ion, but I also don't think he cared one way or the other. If he did, I'm pretty sure he wouldn't have let you see the kids, no matter what I said." She looked up as Patrick and a tall, dark-haired man approached the table.

Ion rose to his feet. "I'm Ion Vasile. You must be Adrien's friend."

"Yes, I'm Goran Isovanich. I'm pleased to meet you. I'm happy that Adrien seems to have found a man he can care about." Goran shook Ion's hand then motioned to the table. "Let's sit and we'll discuss what I've learned."

* * * *

An hour later, Ion's head swam with all the information, but he was happy to know that the doctors at Mount Sinai Queens had done everything they could for Bogdan. Goren would monitor his progress, but he didn't feel like there was any reason why he needed to stay around.

"I appreciate everything you've done, Mr Isovanich," Olive said as they stood and shook hands.

"My pleasure, Mrs Vasile. Adrien has never asked me to help out before, and I'm more than willing to do a favor for a friend." Goran bowed slightly over her hand before he turned to Ion. "It was nice to meet you as well, Ion. I'll call Adrien when I get to the airport."

"Do you need a ride there? I'd be happy to drive you," Patrick offered, his eyes gleaming.

Ion hid his smile. Goran was totally Patrick's type, and his friend would be more than willing to drive Goran to the airport or let the man take him for a ride. The way the surgeon was eyeing him, Patrick's wishes just might come true.

"I would love a ride, Mr Gaverson," Goran practically purred and Olive shot Ion a quick roll of the eyes.

After saying goodbye to Goran and Patrick, Ion and Olive went back up to Bogdan's room. They sat for a little while then Ion started to fidget, unable to stay still. He wanted to pace, but knew it would bother Olive and Bogdan if he did.

Finally, Olive stuck out her leg to nudge his foot. "Why don't you go home or to work for a little while? You can come back to sit with him when I go to pick up the kids from school."

"Are you sure?"

"Honey, there's nothing either of us can do for him except sit and stare. He might be unconscious, but I have to think he can feel us looking at him and it has to be a little unnerving." She giggled and he chuckled.

"You're right. Okay. I'm going. Text me when you need to leave and I'll head back over." He hugged her before he left.

He flagged down a cab and headed to his place to change into the right kind of clothes for work. On the way, he texted Adrien to let him know that he was coming into the office for a little while. Ion also grabbed some of his business books, planning on doing some studying while at the hospital later that day.

* * * *

Ion had been working on his project for an hour when he got a call from Adrien.

"Why don't you come up to my office, Mr Vasile?"

A little startled by Adrien's formal tone, Ion hesitated before he said, "Certainly, sir. I'll be right up."

He secured his computer and files then went up to the executive floor. Mr Richardson's secretary was seated at Patrick's desk. *She must be filling in for Patrick while Richardson's out of town.*

"Mr Bellamy wanted me to come up for a meeting," he said when she glanced up.

She motioned for him to enter. "You can go right on in. He's expecting you."

"Thank you."

Ion knocked then waited to hear Adrien say 'come in' before he entered. He shut the door behind him before leaning against it to watch Adrien walk across the room to him. Protesting never crossed his mind as Adrien embraced him.

Sighing, he encircled Adrien's waist and rested his head on the broad shoulder in front of him. "I'm not sure I can deal with this much longer."

Adrien nuzzled his hair. "I know, honey, but you're stronger than you think and you'll deal with all of this shit because Olive needs you."

"She doesn't have any other family. Her parents are both gone and she was an only child. I don't know if I should keep going there so that my parents can be there with her."

He didn't fight as Adrien moved him a few inches away so he could meet his gaze. As much as he wanted to close his eyes, he didn't, allowing Adrien to study him.

"Olive wants you with her, Ion. If she didn't, she'd tell you. I trust her to know her own mind and maybe she isn't as tight with your parents as you think." Adrien surprised him by leaning in and rubbing their noses together. "Come sit down and tell me what happened with your mom. Oh, and I let my mother know that you would be at the hospital this evening if she wanted to stop by, though I wouldn't put it past her to go and meet Olive."

Ion lifted his eyebrows at the thought of elegant Alyssa Bellamy chatting with his middle-class, housewife sister-in-law. Yet he had the feeling that they could be good friends because they were the same kind of strong women.

"Is Patrick coming back in today?"

Adrien snorted. "He called to ask for the entire day off. I get the feeling something came up after he left the hospital."

"Something did come up, but it was at the hospital." Ion flopped into the couch set against the wall.

"Oh really? Do tell."

"You have seen what Goran Isovanich looks like right?"

Adrien dropped next to him and shook his head. "You're kidding me? Goran and Patrick? That must be why Goran called to let me know that he would be staying in town for the weekend. I'll ask to see if he'll want to join us tomorrow night."

Ion scooted down on the cushions until his head rested on the back one and he stared at the ceiling. "Should we be going out?"

"Yes. You can spend however much time at the hospital tomorrow during the day, but we won't be going out until eight or nine that night and you won't be there then." Adrien rested his hand on Ion's knee. "I know you want to be there for your brother, but until they start bringing him out of the coma, there's nothing you can do."

He exhaled slowly, knowing Adrien was right. Olive had said they weren't planning on bringing Bogdan out until next week, so all he'd be doing would be staring at his brother lying in his hospital bed. Besides, he'd been looking forward to dancing and relaxing with Adrien.

"You're right. Did you want to check with Goran or should I call Patrick to see if they'll be joining us at the club?"

"I'll call Goran. It isn't often I get to tease him about his personal life. He tends to be a monk most of the time because of his practice and his *pro bono* work." Adrien squeezed Ion's knee once before he stood to stroll over to his desk. "I'm glad he and Patrick are hitting it off, though I still think Winston would be a better fit for Patrick."

"Oh, don't worry about it. Let them have their fun, but Goran will go back to wherever he's from and Patrick will be looking for another guy."

"True. They both need to let loose a little bit. Goran isn't the type of guy to forget his work for too long. He must have a free weekend, which is why he could check your brother and hang out with Patrick." Adrien scrolled through his email.

"Was there something you wanted to talk to me about aside from my parents? Whom I don't want to discuss at the moment," he informed him.

Adrien's lips lifted in a small smile. "No. I just wanted to give you a hug. You can go back to work. Did you want to catch a ride with me or are you going straight to the hospital when you're done here?"

"Olive is going to let me know when she's leaving to get the kids. I'm going to sit with Bogdan while she's gone, so I'll head right there." He pushed to his feet then stretched.

Adrien watched him and Ion shivered a little at the heat in his eyes. God, he wanted to go and strip Adrien before taking the man deep inside his body, but it wasn't the time and definitely not the place for that. So he blew Adrien a kiss before he left.

He managed to focus on his work until Olive got a hold of him then he let Mr Herner know that he was leaving. Ion sent Adrien a short message that he was going to the hospital. When he got to his brother's room, there hadn't been any change in his condition except that the swelling seemed to have gone down a little bit, which was good news.

Ion settled in to do some studying while he kept his silent brother company.

Chapter Nine

"Holy fuck," Adrien breathed as Ion walked out of his bathroom.

Ion winked at him while strolling over to where his boots sat. Adrien couldn't believe Ion could breathe or bend, considering how tight his jeans were. There was no doubt about what Ion was packing and a shot of jealousy rushed through Adrien at the thought of anyone seeing his lover like that.

The dark blue T-shirt Ion wore lovingly hugged every muscle and ridge of Ion's chest and stomach. Plus, it rode up just a little to expose his tanned skin, causing Adrien's hands to itch to touch him.

"I'm not sure I want to go out any more," he muttered, staring at Ion's ass very obviously on display when the man bent over.

"What are you talking about?" Ion glanced at him under his arm as he tied his boots. "You were the one who said this was a good idea. We all need to relax after the week we had."

"I know, but I wasn't taking into consideration how fuckable you'd look in your club clothes," he admitted, willing to let Ion see his jealousy.

"Oh, how sweet. Is the green-eyed monster rearing its ugly head?" Ion straightened before sauntering toward Adrien, letting his hips swing a little more than usual.

Adrien's mouth went dry and he gripped Ion's waist then brought their groins together. Ion wiggled for a second and Adrien groaned as lust shot through him to pool in his cock and balls.

"It's not that monster rearing its head," he confessed, sliding his hands around to grab handfuls of Ion's butt. "I'm not sure I'm going to survive dancing with you."

Ion's warm breath bathed his cheek before he kissed him softly. They kissed and cuddled for a few minutes until Adrien knew they had to stop or they'd be doing some horizontal dancing on the couch. He wrapped his hands around Ion to crush him tightly to his body while catching his breath.

"We need to get going," he reminded Ion.

"Are you sure you're up to this?" Ion joked. "Can you control yourself or will I be getting fucked in the bathroom at the club?"

It had been a long time since he'd done that and he was too old now. He pinched Ion's ass before going to grab his keys and wallets. "Not tonight, honey. I want to make love to you in our bed, not up against some wall like a quick lay. We need to get going. Goran and Patrick are meeting us at the restaurant."

"Where did you decide we're going to eat?" Ion joined him, holding out his own wallet for Adrien to carry, since there was obviously no room to fit it in his pockets.

Adrien tucked them away then gestured for Ion to go out in front of him. "We're meeting them at John's of 12th Street. Thought a little Italian would be good to get energy for the night."

"I love that place." Ion grinned as they waited for the elevator.

"I do too. Goran's never eaten there. Plus it's not that far away from the club, so we won't have too long a car ride." Adrien rested his hand at the small of Ion's back, teasing him with soft strokes of his fingers under the hem of Ion's shirt.

"Is Daniel driving us?" Ion leaned into his touch.

"Only to the restaurant. We'll cab it from there. Oh, and Sidney's going to meet us at the club."

Daniel had the car waiting for them at the curb and they climbed in. Adrien let Ion chatter about anything he wanted. It didn't have to be important or earth shattering—he simply wanted to listen to Ion talk because he loved the sound of his voice.

He brought Ion close to him, holding him tight as they drove through the darkening city streets. Ion fell silent as well, seeming to enjoy just being in Adrien's company. They moved apart as the car came to a stop outside the restaurant.

When they walked into the place, Adrien looked around to see if Goran and Patrick were there, and spotted their friends sitting at a corner table. He waved to let them know he'd seen them then directed Ion toward them.

"It's good to see you, Goran. I'm glad you and Patrick were able to drag yourselves out of bed to join us," he joked as they took their seats.

"Fuck you, Adrien," Goran replied, but there wasn't any heat in his tone. He was sitting so close to Patrick, they could be sharing a chair.

Blushing, Patrick ducked his head for a second then raised it to look at Adrien. "I guess you've never slept with Goran or you'd realize how difficult it was for us to get our asses out of bed."

Adrien chuckled. "I thought about it once when we first met at Oxford, but then decided it was better that we be friends and not lovers. He's a little more Alpha than I want to deal with."

"Meaning I'm pig-headed and always believe I am right. Which is kind of like a God complex and it makes me a good surgeon." Goran stroked his fingers over Patrick's cheek then grinned at Ion. "It's nice to see you again, Ion. I hope your brother is doing well."

Ion nodded. "Yes. They've made the decision to start bringing him out of the coma on Monday."

"Wonderful news." Goran motioned toward the bottle of wine on the table. "I took the liberty of ordering wine for us."

"Thank you."

Adrien enjoyed dinner as he and Goran shared college stories. Ion and Patrick matched them with their own tales. He saw the heat between Patrick and his friend, but it was a lust that would burn out eventually if they were to stay together. Adrien could tell because it was totally different from what he felt for Ion.

Turning to look at his lover, his heart literally skipped a beat when Ion threw his head back and laughed. There was so much joy and life in that sound. All he wanted to do was embrace him and hold him close to his chest. He wanted to wake up every morning and see Ion in the bed beside him. Coming home from work every night with Ion to cook dinner or even to go out.

Taking Ion sailing down the coast in his boat had become one of Adrien's wishes. He'd have to do that some weekend to help Ion relax after all of the drama of his brother's accident and his parents' rejection. He'd have to see which weekend coming up would work best for Ion.

The food was great and the company entertaining, so there was no doubt once they finished eating they would be going on to the club. Adrien got them a cab so they could get to Wander without any trouble. Ion called him a snob, but Adrien didn't like using public transportation.

Oh, it wasn't the fact that the less fortunate used it or anything like that. He just didn't think it was particularly safe, especially at night, and he wasn't going to risk anything happening to Ion.

There was a line of men waiting to get into Wander when they arrived, but Adrien led the other three to the front and the bouncer let them in with a nod.

"Do you know the owner or something?" Ion muttered as they were escorted to a VIP section in the back of the club, where Sidney already waited for them.

"Yes, I do actually." He pointed at his best friend. "It's one of Sidney's side ventures. He likes to find interesting ways to invest his money and working for me isn't as exciting as one would think."

"Who would ever think that?" Ion winked as they joined Sidney.

"I don't know. I find my work very rewarding." Adrien gave Sidney a one-arm hug and pounded on his back. "Glad you made it back all right. You remember Goran, right?"

"Yes. Good seeing you again, Goran. Gentlemen, you obviously came to dance while we older gentlemen have come to ogle you." Sidney shook Goran's hand and glanced at Patrick and Ion.

Ion kissed Adrien then grabbed Patrick's hand. "Order me a drink, love. Let's go."

Adrien dropped into a chair next to Sidney then motioned to the waiter hovering just to the side of the VIP area. He ordered drinks for all of them and once that was taken care of, he turned to look at Sidney.

"How long have you been here?"

Sidney seemed to have to pull his gaze away from someone at the bar. "For an hour or so. I came to go over the books and stuff with the manager then just relaxed while I waited for you." His gaze went back to its original spot.

"See something you like?" Adrien nudged him with an elbow.

"What?" Sidney frowned.

Goran snorted. "I think you're busy checking out that tattooed bartender. The one with the guy liner and pierced ears."

As Sidney sputtered in protest, Adrien turned to try and spot the man Goran talked about. Unfortunately, the crowd had grown too big around that section, so he couldn't see anything.

"I'll have to take a walk later on to see this man who has caught your attention so completely." He wiggled his eyebrows as he threatened.

Sidney leaned over to punch his arm. "Don't do anything stupid. I'm not interested in anyone, especially not a tattooed pierced bartender who probably takes a new guy home every night."

Adrien blinked at the bitterness in Sidney's voice. *What brought that on? Has something happen that I'm not aware of?* He swore he'd grab Sidney for lunch one day next week to figure out what the hell was going on.

Goran whistled low, bringing Adrien's attention to the two men dancing just a few feet away from them. He grunted when he realized it was Ion and Patrick. *Christ!* Ion moved like he was having sex on the dance floor. The thrust of Ion's hips and wiggle of his ass caused Adrien to stiffen. He swore, wishing he had worn looser clothing.

"Makes you wish you'd worn sweats, huh?" Goran murmured.

Adrien nodded, not sure he could get his mouth to move as lust swamped him. If this was how he felt after only a few minutes of watching Ion, he might just break his rule about not having sex in the bathroom.

"I have a private room upstairs," Sidney suggested. His grin was evil.

"I might take you up on that," Adrien said before he drank his shot then jumped to his feet. "I think I'm going to do some dancing."

He didn't like the way some of the other dancers were checking his lover out. Adrien wanted to stake his claim and make sure they knew Ion was off limits. After stalking up to Ion, he slid his arm around Ion's waist then jerked him against him.

Ion didn't even blink an eye. He entwined his body around Adrien's, rubbing and grinding until Adrien thought he would come in his jeans. He hadn't done that since he was a teenager and wasn't about to do it now. When the song faded into a different one, he turned to look at Sidney who was already tossing him a key. His friend pointed to a door in the closest wall.

"Where are we going?" Ion asked breathlessly as Adrien dragged him from the floor.

"Somewhere I can fuck you without everyone watching us," he informed him.

"Oh thank God. I was hoping you'd break down and do me, but I have to admit I didn't really want to have sex in the bathroom. Not a lot of room and I don't like the idea of people walking in on us." Ion chuckled. "Guess I'm not an exhibitionist."

Adrien stuck the key in the lock then jiggled it until it opened. He flicked the lights on and saw the flight of stairs leading up to a second floor. He patted Ion's ass, encouraging him to go on up while Adrien made sure the door was secure. He didn't think anyone came up here except for Sidney, but he wasn't taking a risk.

"Wow. Sidney has quite the little love nest up here," Ion said and Adrien hurried to see what Ion was talking about.

The king-sized bed took up most of the space, but there was a small cabinet and a mini fridge there as well. Ion was looking through the cabinet and crowed. Adrien saw him hold up a tube of lube.

"No condoms anymore since our tests came back negative. Sidney must get his pick of the men downstairs. Instead of risking a more serious connection that could happen if he takes them home, he brings them up here, fucks them and sends them on their way." Adrien shook his head as he glanced around. "Sidney's always been shy of commitment. Male or female."

"Let's not talk about your friend, huh? I want your cock in my ass ASAP."

When he looked back at Ion, he blinked. How the hell had Ion got naked that quickly? Ion sprawled on the bed, spread eagle, and stroking his cock while fingering his ass. The open slick was next to him on the bed.

Adrien couldn't take his eyes away as he stripped as fast as he could, throwing his clothes in every direction before he dove onto the mattress. After kneeling between Ion's legs, he reached for the lube.

"Oh, God. I need you, Adrien. I'm primed to come as soon as you shove your dick in," Ion babbled.

He coated his cock then used the extra lube to ease two of his fingers in besides Ion's two. Ion's body welcomed him like it had been built for him, which in his heart, Adrien couldn't help believing was true.

Ion arched his hips off the bed while they stretched his body until neither one of them could wait any longer. Adrien removed their fingers then positioned himself at Ion's opening. With one long, smooth thrust, Adrien buried himself deep.

"Fuck," he shouted before draping Ion's legs over his arms then reaming Ion's ass. "You're so fucking tight and perfect for my cock. I love taking you."

Moaning, Ion braced his hands against the headboard and pushed back, countering each one of Ion's moves with one of his own. Adrien knew Ion was on the edge, but he wasn't ready to let him go, so he reached out and wrapped his fingers around the base of Ion's length.

"Adrien," Ion protested then whined when Adrien tilted his hips enough to nail Ion's gland. "You're being mean. I want to come. Please."

"We're going to come together, so you can't until I do," Adrien ordered.

He played Ion's body like he'd learned all the man's secrets, yet he knew they could make love for years and he'd always find new things to make Ion moan. The steady thump of the bass from the club under them helped provide the perfect rhythm for fucking.

As the pressure built, Adrien let go of Ion's cock, knowing that as soon as Ion came, he would as well. Ion yelled and Adrien cried out as the muscles surrounding his shaft clamped down on him to the point of pain.

Cum shot from Ion, painting his stomach and even his chest. Adrien rocked almost all the way out, then slammed back in before he came as well. He flooded Ion with his seed, loving the idea of marking Ion as his.

Once the last drop seemed to be drained from him, he collapsed to the side while Ion winced as he slid out. Their pants filled the air as he tried to catch his breath. Finally, he rolled onto his elbow to stare down at Ion.

"Move in with me," he said.

Ion jerked his stare from the ceiling to Adrien's face. "Are you serious?"

"Yes. I don't like the idea of us being apart for any length of time except work and school. I want to share my bed with you, wake up beside you and take a shower with you in the morning. I want your clothes in my closet and your shoes next to mine on the floor."

"You have to do this here? In an upstairs love nest at a gay club after you've just fucked me silly and your cum is dripping from my ass?" Ion shook his head. "You couldn't have thought of a more romantic place to do it at?"

Well yes, he could've done it more romantically, but it wouldn't have been any more honest and sincere. He wanted Ion living with him for all those reasons he'd listed.

"If you want, I'll take you out to dinner tomorrow, give you flowers and a beautiful box with a gold copy of my key in it. But I couldn't help it, Ion. I love you so much and it just came out." Adrien rested his hand on Ion's chest, trailing his fingers through the cum then bringing them to his mouth to taste.

Ion studied him and Adrien grew worried. *Is it too soon? Should he have waited for them to have dated a month or a year?*

"I know we haven't been dating for very long, but I know, in my heart, this is the right thing for us, Ion." He took Ion's hand in his then pressed it to his heart. "I love you, but if you're not ready to do this, then we won't. I'm not going to push you into anything you don't want to do."

Ion took a deep breath then curled up to take Adrien's lips in a hard kiss. When they finished, he lay back down. "Of course I'll move in with you. I know how you feel about it being right. I'm sure our friends and family will think we're crazy to do this so quickly, but when it feels this real, then we should do as our hearts tell us."

Adrien tackled Ion, kissing and hugging him until they were both breathless. Ion shoved him over onto his back then grabbed the lube from where he'd tossed it earlier. He groaned when Ion slicked up his cock once again before straddling his hips. He put his hands at Ion's waist, steadying him as he impaled himself on Adrien's shaft.

This time he kept their love making slow and gentle. He wasn't interested in chasing Ion over the edge into passion. He wanted to ease both of them into their climaxes and Ion seemed to feel the same. They rocked together, kissing and touching, letting the pleasure build.

His balls tightened and it was the only warning he had before he came, filling Ion with his cum once again. Ion released a low moan and pearly strings of cum coated Adrien's stomach. A few seconds later, Ion fell into his arms. Adrien ignored the stickiness between them as he held Ion close.

He didn't know how much time had gone by before Ion sighed then climbed off him.

"We should get back down there and celebrate. Also, let Patrick and Sidney know they're going to have to help me move my stuff to your place." Ion rummaged through the cabinet and came up with some wet wipes.

They cleaned up as best they could then dressed. Adrien went down first to unlock the door while Ion finished wiggling into his jeans. Once Ion was with him, they slipped from the stairway out into the milling group of men. It seemed to have grown more crowded and was louder.

Adrien took Ion's hand in his as he led the way back to where their friends were drinking and dancing. He couldn't wait to tell everyone he knew that Ion was moving in with him. Plus his family would be thrilled to know he wasn't letting Ion get away. Of course, once his mother heard about their new living arrangements, she was going to start nagging him about getting married. He smiled. Who knew getting the right to marry would become such a hassle?

Chapter Ten

Ion glanced around their apartment, making sure everything looked perfect. Bogdan and Olive were coming for dinner for the first time since Ion had moved in with Adrien. It had been four months since then, and Bogdan was still recovering from his accident.

He'd come out of the coma without any brain damage, which was a miracle in itself, but aside from the shattered leg and arm, he didn't seem to have sustained anything lasting from being in the hospital for three months. Bogdan was doing rehab for his injuries and Olive had stayed strong to help him.

They'd never discussed the fact that Ion and his parents hadn't spoken a word since that day in the hospital. Olive kept him informed of how they were doing, but Ion wasn't going to be the one to break the standoff.

He was who he was, and he wasn't going to apologize for loving Adrien. Olive had never asked him to be any different, and Bogdan had been focused on other things besides what was going on between Ion and their parents.

Glancing at the clock, he wondered if Adrien would make it home. His lover had had to go to Japan to deal with some business issues. He'd thought he'd be back yesterday, but his flight had gotten delayed.

Oh well. If he's not here, it'll be okay. I'll just have them over again when Adrien can be here. Just as Ion thought that, the door opened and Adrien entered.

"You made it," he said as he went to give him a kiss and take his jacket. "You have enough time to take a shower and change your clothes."

Adrien gave him a tired smile and nod before heading to their bedroom. He heard the shower turn on just as the buzzer sounded.

"Yes, Guilleme?"

"Mr Vasile, your brother and sister-in-law are here," the doorman informed him.

"You can send them up," he confirmed then glanced around one more time before he went into the kitchen to open the wine. Bogdan couldn't drink alcohol at the moment, so he and Ion would be having coffee or tea. He peered into the oven to double check that the lasagna he'd made was just about ready to come out.

A knock sounded and Ion rushed to the door then threw it open. "Welcome."

His smile dimmed slightly when he saw his father standing beside Bogdan. Olive took his hand before stepping inside, which forced Ion to move back.

"I hope you don't mind. Mama is visiting Aunt Sallem and Pops would be by himself. You know he can't cook." Olive used her eyes to plead with him.

"Pops is welcome here whenever he wants. There's enough food for everyone. Adrien just got back from a business trip, so he's cleaning up and will be out in a few minutes." He gestured to their coats. "Can I take your jackets?"

He took Olive's and his father's then waited patiently while Bogdan took his off. No one offered to help him. His brother was very determined to get back to the way he was before the accident.

"You can either go on into the living room or the kitchen. There's some merlot breathing on the counter and I just made a pot of coffee." He hung up their coats then gestured toward the other rooms.

"Why don't Bogdan and I got get the drinks? You can show Pops to the living room," Olive suggested as she took her husband by the arm to lead him to the kitchen.

Ion shook his head, but looked at his father and gave him a small smile. "Come on. You'll love the living room. Adrien has a fifty-two inch television and watching games is pretty incredible on it."

Pops grunted before saying, "George from the factory has one. He had us over for a ball game the other weekend. Looked good."

Well, if this isn't awkward. It wasn't like we had a lot to talk about before. Now it's like there's a giant elephant in the room and it has Mama's name on it.

After motioning to the couch, he took a seat in one of the chairs. He rested his hands on his thighs while he wondered what they could talk about. His father cleared his throat and Ion looked at him. Pops studied him for a moment before looking around the room.

"I'm sorry we haven't talked for a while, Ion. I know that must seem like we've disowned you and to be honest, I think your mother has."

Pain shot through Ion's chest, even though he shouldn't have been surprised by his father's announcement. "What about you?"

His father shrugged. "I don't suppose it matters whether you love a guy or a girl. Do you love this man?"

"Yes, Pops. I do love him." He wasn't going to lie to make his father comfortable, but it sounded like maybe he didn't have to worry about that.

"And he loves you?"

"I do," Adrien spoke from where he stood in the doorway. He strolled over to sit on the arm of the chair and rest his hand on Ion's shoulder. "I love your son with all my heart, Mr Vasile."

"Then that's all that matters." His father held out his hand to Adrien. "Welcome to the family, Mr Bellamy."

"Please, call me Adrien. I have to ask what will your wife say to all this?" Adrien shook Pops' hand before going back to sit next to Ion.

"She's not happy with what I think. Your mother has called me many names that we won't discuss here. I've told her that she doesn't have to have anything to do with you if that's how she feels, but I won't turn my back on my youngest son because of this."

Tears welled in Ion's eyes and he wanted to hug him, but even if his father accepted who he loved, Pops wasn't a demonstrative man, so hugging wasn't an option.

"Thank you, Pops."

Another shrug told Ion he was a little uncomfortable with the emotions brewing in the room. At that moment, Olive and Bogdan came in. She carried a tray with the wine glasses and coffee cup and his brother brought in a plate of appetizers Ion had made up beforehand.

Everyone got settled and they were chatting quite happily when someone knocked on the door. Ion looked over at Adrien quizzically and his lover shrugged, yet he had the feeling Adrien knew who it was.

Opening the door, Ion was shocked to see Robert and Alyssa along with Amelia and Jonathon all standing there.

"Umm...hello. I didn't know you were going to be in the city this weekend," he said as they walked in.

They hung up their own coats then went on to be introduced to Olive, Bogdan and Ion's father. Adrien joined him in the kitchen as he gathered more glasses and opened another bottle of wine.

"Did you know they were going to stop by?" he hissed as he checked the vegetables roasting in the oven along with the lasagna.

"They said they might stop by if they decided to come in. Nothing was definite. Don't worry. We have more than enough for everyone. And if they're still hungry, they'll stop somewhere to get more food." Adrien nuzzled his cheek and patted his ass before strolling back into the living room with the rest of the wine.

It turned out to be the evening Ion had dreamed would happen. Somehow his father and Robert got along beautifully. Ion hadn't known how much his father loved car racing, and that was perfect for Robert.

Amelia and Alyssa chatted with Olive and Bogdan like they were old friends. Adrien put his arm around Ion's shoulder and he turned to press his face against Adrien's flat stomach. Taking a deep breath, he got his emotions under control enough to be able to talk with everyone without bursting into tears.

The only way it would have been better was if his mother had been there, yet he had a feeling that even if she had accepted his being gay, she wouldn't have been happy with the Bellamys. Their money would have convinced her that they were looking down on her because she didn't live in the Hamptons or own a huge house. She would've found something wrong because she wasn't a happy person if she wasn't the one who was the center of attention.

Ion pushed any thought of his mother to the back of his mind. He wasn't going to let her ruin his happiness on a wonderful night with family all around him.

Dinner was great and after they finished eating, they gathered again in the living room to continue talking. Ion went to sit next to Bogdan who wasn't talking much but seemed to be enjoying himself.

"Are you doing all right?" he asked as he sat.

Bogdan nodded. "Just tired. All of this is a little overwhelming."

"I know. I'm sorry. I didn't realize Adrien's family was going to stop by. If I had, I would've warned you. They're marvelous people, but they can be a little much at times."

"Do they come over often?" Bogdan waved his hand in their direction.

Ion shook his head. "No. In fact, this is the first time they've visited us since I moved in here. I wonder why they came to the city."

"Ion, can you come here for a moment? I might be able to tell you why my family is here." Adrien held out his hand.

Ion went to his love, wondering what Adrien was talking about. "You said you didn't know they were going to be here."

"I lied. I asked them to come and join us tonight. I knew that Olive and Bogdan would be here. Having your father here is a bonus."

Ion clenched his hands and watched in shock as Adrien dropped to one knee in front of everyone. He thought his eyes would fall out of his head if they opened any wider when Adrien pulled a small blue box out of his pocket.

"Ion Vasile, love of my life, will you marry me and put me out of my misery?"

He snorted in surprised laughter at Adrien's question. "Out of your misery?"

"If I have to listen to my mother ask me one more time when I'm going to marry you so she can start planning the wedding, I think I'll go crazy," Adrien murmured, motioning with his head to where Alyssa stood, fingers pressed to her mouth and tears in her eyes.

"Well, when you put it that way," Ion said as he closed the distance between them while Adrien stood. He wrapped his arms around Adrien's neck and whispered against his lips, "I love you, Adrien Bellamy, and yes, I'll marry you whenever and wherever you want."

About the Author

There is beauty in every kind of love, so why not live a life without boundaries? Experiencing everything the world offers fascinates TA and writing about the things that make each of us unique is how she shares those insights. When not writing, TA's watching movies, reading and living life to the fullest.

T.A. Chase loves to hear from readers. You can find her contact information, website details and author profile page at http://www.totallybound.com.

Totally Bound Publishing